THE WALLFLOWER'S MIDNIGHT WALTZ

WALTZING WITH WALLFLOWERS (BOOK 2)

ROSE PEARSON

© Copyright 2024 by Rose Pearson - All rights reserved.

In no way is it legal to reproduce, duplicate, or transmit any part of this document by either electronic means or in printed format. Recording of this publication is strictly prohibited and any storage of this document is not allowed unless with written permission from the publisher. All rights reserved.

Respective author owns all copyrights not held by the publisher.

THE WALLFLOWER'S
MIDNIGHT WALTZ

PROLOGUE

"This has been an excellent first Season, I think."
Lady Alice Chambers laughed and slipped her arm through her mother's.

"Mama, we have only been here for three weeks. I hardly think that we can call such a short time a success."

"Yes, but you have had a great many gentlemen calling on you, have you not?" Lady Talbot smiled at her daughter, and there was a glimmer of satisfaction hidden within it, though Alice could not blame her for that. After all, her mother had done everything in her power to make certain that Alice was ready for the coming Season, and it was thanks to her that Alice was having such a success. Her afternoons had been filled with gentleman callers, her nights with being pulled out to dance by both old and new acquaintances. As yet, no gentleman had stood out to her, none had caught her eye in particular, but there did not seem to be any real urgency for her to choose only one. There was time, perhaps even a second Season, before she would have to make such a decision.

"And there have been many gentlemen eager to make your acquaintance. At every ball we attend, you have at least five new acquaintances within the first hour!"

Alice smiled and nodded, but turned her gaze back to the path rather than looking up at her mother. The sun was warm, the gentle wind whispering through the trees of St James' Park and, though she was contented, there was no true satisfaction in her heart. Yes, she had many gentlemen calling on her and many more who were eager to acquaint themselves with her, but her heart told her to be cautious. After all, such gentlemen were certainly eager and made her glad of their interest in her, but at the same time, Alice recognized that her standing as the daughter of an Earl, as well as her substantial dowry, was reason enough for some gentlemen to seek out her company. She did not want to draw close to a gentleman whose only interest in her was her father's fortune. There had to be a true connection between them, true interest and genuine consideration between them, before she would even *think* about forming a strong attachment.

I only hope Mama understands.

Biting her lip, Alice looked away as her mother continued to speak at length of all the different gentlemen who had come to call on Alice of late. There had never been any discussion with her mother about the sort of gentleman she might wed. To Alice's mind, such a conversation was important, but she had never once broached the subject with her mother – and nor had her mother done so with her!

Perhaps she ought to do so now.

"There are gentlemen who will only be eager for my

company because of my dowry, however," she began as her mother snorted and rolled her eyes. "I should like to be cautious when it comes to considering the gentlemen who come to call. I do not want to form an attachment with any gentleman who wishes to marry me solely for the dowry I will bring to the marriage – and for whatever else Father will give me per year."

Lady Talbot laughed and waved her hand vaguely.

"I do not think you need to concern yourself in that yet, my dear girl. In time, mayhap, for once a gentleman seeks to court you, your father and I will do all we can to make certain that he is both suitable and financially settled."

A weight lifted from Alice's shoulders.

"Thank you, Mama. I am glad to know that. I–" Seeing a lady coming towards them, Alice stopped her conversation, ready to greet the lady in question. "Good afternoon, Lady Glenforth. Where is Lady Violet today?"

Much to her astonishment, Lady Glenforth not only ignored her, but also lifted her chin, turned her head and walked away with quick, hurried steps, as though the only thing she wanted to do was get away from Alice and her mother as quickly as she could.

"Lady Glenforth?" Pausing in their walk, Lady Talbot turned and called after her friend, but the lady did not so much as glance over her shoulder at them. "Goodness, did she just give us the cut direct?"

Alice nodded, biting her lip.

"I am afraid that she did, Mama."

"But why?" Lady Talbot's face had gone very white

indeed, her face now devoid of color as she gripped Alice's hand tightly. "What have we done?"

A tendril of fear began to wrap around Alice's heart.

"I do not know. I cannot think of anything."

"We were at the ball last evening and nothing untoward happened." Lady Talbot's eyes rounded as she looked at Alice. "Unless something occurred that you did not tell me about?"

"Nothing happened, I promise!" A little upset at her mother's response, Alice took her hand away from her mother's tight grip. "I danced with a different gentleman for every dance and returned to your side in the interim. That is all!"

Nodding slowly, Lady Talbot looked away, her lips pursing for a few seconds.

"Yes, I suppose that is true."

"So I have done nothing, as you must be aware," Alice continued, as Lady Talbot closed her eyes tightly and took a deep breath. "Something else has happened. Mayhap… mayhap we should return to the carriage and thence home. Father might know something of it." Lady Talbot's eyes flared, and she caught her breath, one hand going to her heart. "What is wrong?" Her own heart beginning to quicken now with a mixture of fear and concern, Alice took a step closer to her mother, catching her arm. "Mama, what is wrong?"

"Your… your father." Lady Talbot closed her eyes. "Surely it cannot be! He…" Her gaze moved away for a few moments, turning to the view behind Alice's shoulder and lingering there as her words came to a close. Alice wanted to ask her mother what it was Lord Talbot might have done, but the words would not come, the fear in her heart holding the words back. "Come."

Without warning, Lady Talbot turned on her heel and strode back along the path towards the waiting carriage, leaving Alice to hurry after her. She walked more quickly than Alice had ever seen her do before, and by the time they reached the carriage, they were both breathing heavily. Silence reigned as they were driven home, and though Alice tried several times to start a conversation with her mother, her words were either left to be swallowed by the silence, or only acknowledged with a brief nod or quiet murmur. Nothing but her fear remained, and it began to overwhelm her, taking over every part of her, burning through her until she could barely contain it. Twisting her fingers together, Alice looked out of the window at the familiar streets, fearful of what they were going to discover when they reached home. If Lady Glenforth had given them the cut direct – something so severe as that – then it could only be on account of something significant, though what that significance might be, Alice could not even begin to imagine. Her heart ached for her mother, who sat so quietly, with her hands at her lap, her head bowed and a paleness to her skin which had not been there before Lady Glenforth had walked past them. Would she recover from this, whatever it was? Alice did not think that she had ever seen her mother look so distressed before.

"My Lady."

The footman opened the door, and Lady Talbot was out of the carriage in the very next moment, with Alice following quickly behind. Hurrying into the townhouse –

and a little uncertain as to whether or not she ought to be following, Alice went after her mother as she made her way directly to the study, pushing open the door and immediately throwing questions at her husband.

"What have you done, Talbot? What is it that has been discovered?"

Standing in the doorway, Alice looked across at her father, but her fear did not diminish in any way. Rather, it grew so forceful that she wrapped her arms around her waist in an attempt to bring even a small measure of comfort.

Lord Talbot put his head in his hands and groaned aloud, though Lady Talbot merely strode across to the desk and thumped one hand down on the table.

"Tell me! Lady Glenforth gave us the cut direct, so something must have occurred! What is it?"

Alice put one hand to her mouth as her father slowly lifted his head to look at her mother. His eyes were bloodshot, his skin grey, his shoulders drooping – and when he spoke, his voice rasped and tore.

"I have been discovered." Closing his eyes, he let out a heavy sigh. "I have not been the sort of gentleman I ought to have been. I have spent money on... on dark things. I have lost a great deal of coin in gambling dens. In short, my dear, I am disgraced."

Alice slumped back against the doorframe while her mother stood, frozen in place as she stared down at her husband. The truth had come out and made itself known in all its ugliness, in its dark and twisted form, and now its shadow was spreading out across them all. It was her father's disgrace but, as Alice well knew, the disgrace of her father would be attached to her mother and also to her.

At that moment, the realization that all of society would turn its back on her ran over Alice like a drenching cold rain, washing away all of her hopes and expectations in one frozen moment. Closing her eyes, she let out a sob and, turning from the room, ran far from it as though escaping the study might take some of the darkness from her.

But it did not. Instead, it followed her, wrapping itself around her shoulders and clinging to her just as it would do from now on. Weeping, Alice threw herself onto her bed and let the tears fall as her heart broke.

Society would push her away now, would regard her as less than nothing.

Now, she had no hope whatsoever.

CHAPTER ONE

*A*lice closed her eyes.
"I do not think this is a good idea."

"What else is there for us to do?" Lady Talbot smiled tightly, though the smile did not reach her eyes. "You cannot sit at home for another Season, I will not have it! It is much too sorrowful there, much too hopeless."

"Just as it is here," Alice murmured, looking out across the ballroom, and wondering how many ladies and gentlemen present would remember her father and what had been revealed about him only last Season.

No doubt almost all of them would, for news of her father's failings had spread quickly through society last Season, forcing them to return to the estate where they had hidden away for almost an entire year. Alice had been quite certain that her mother would not permit her to return to London, and had been secretly glad to remain at home, only to be utterly astonished when Lady Talbot had announced her intent for their return – albeit without Lord Talbot himself.

"There will be those who will sympathize." Drawing herself up, Lady Talbot smiled again. "We have been invited here this evening, have we not?"

That was true, Alice had to admit, nodding as her mother took her arm.

"Yes, Mama. It was good of Lord Jennings to invite us."

"His wife, Lady Jennings, and I are good friends. She has written to me a great deal this last year, and I have returned her letters quickly. In fact, she was the one who encouraged me to bring you back to London, telling me that she was quite certain that there would be those amongst society who would not place the blame upon us! Though she did suggest that your father remain at home."

"Which he has done."

Lady Talbot nodded, though there was a darkness in her smile now; a sight which made Alice shiver. From what she knew, her parents were barely speaking to each other. There was silence over the dinner table and, given that her mother retired at the same time as Alice each evening and left Lord Talbot to sit alone, there was not a lot of time for conversation. Lord Talbot had grown thinner, his hair streaked liberally with grey now, and though the estate was doing well, his own strength had certainly diminished.

Alice did not feel particularly sorry for him. After all, the situation which he found himself in was entirely of his own making.

"Now." Lady Talbot said, briskly. "Let us walk around the ballroom. Keep your eyes fixed straight ahead and permit *me* to smile and nod at those around us. That will be a good indicator of those who will be willing to accept both my company *and* yours."

Nervousness washed away all other feelings, and Alice could only nod, falling into step with her mother and doing precisely as asked – walking through the ballroom and keeping her eyes fixed directly ahead.

The whispers, however, she was unable to ignore. There came one or two exclamations as she walked alongside her mother, one or two crass bouts of laughter, and Alice's face began to heat with embarrassment, though she chided herself for such a reaction immediately. It was not *her* shame which had diminished her in the eyes of society, but rather her father's disgrace. It was *his* behavior and not her own which had her in this present state and, though that did not change the response of any of those around her, it brought her a little comfort.

"Ah, Lady Jennings, how grateful I am to you for your welcome."

Alice smiled as the slender lady turned to face both Alice and her mother, reaching out to take Lady Talbot's hand.

"But of course," came the gentle reply. "I am sorry that not everyone has been eager to speak with you or even to greet you! That is not as it ought to be."

As Lady Talbot and Lady Jennings continued their conversation, Alice's attention was caught by the sight of a few young ladies standing together to the side of the ballroom. There were three in conversation together, standing without chaperone or parent near them, and as Alice continued to watch them, she slowly began to realize who they were.

Wallflowers.

A sudden urge to go to join them pulled her close and, with a murmur to her mother, Alice found herself walking towards them. Pressing her lips together, she inclined her head as three faces looked at her, though only one smiled.

"Good evening." Lifting her head, Alice spread her hands a little. "This is not what ought to be done, I know, but I saw you talking together, and my heart has been so very heavy with my lack of companionship, I came to beg you for a little conversation." A flush of embarrassment rose in her chest, but she kept her head lifted regardless. "That does sound most foolish, but it is what I feel. I am certain that you might well be able to understand."

The lady who had been smiling stepped closer.

"You do understand that we are wallflowers, do you not?"

Alice nodded and the smile returned.

"You would take note of us, then? You would wish to speak with three young ladies who are continually overlooked by society?"

She nodded.

"I am one such person also. My father... my father is the Earl of Talbot, and I am Lady Alice."

At this, two of the young ladies looked at each other, though one remained apparently a little confused as to the significance of the name.

"I quite understand," another of the ladies said, smiling. "You are most welcome. I am Lady Frederica."

"And I, Miss Simmons and this is Miss Fairley." The young lady who had been smiling now curtsied before gesturing to the young lady Alice now knew to be Miss Fairley. "Of course you may join us. We all understand what it is to be ignored by society, I can assure you!"

"Even when it is not one's doing!" Lady Frederica exclaimed as Alice nodded fervently. "That is how things stand in your situation also, I think."

"It is!" Alice found herself immediately warming to these three ladies, glad now that she had listened to the instinct that had told her to draw closer. "My father is the one at fault. I do not know all of the details of his indiscretions, but what he *has* said of them is that they were very dark indeed." Gesturing to her mother who, perhaps seeing Alice's action, caught her eye and then smiled, clearly pleased that her daughter had found some companions. "My mother insisted that I come back to London for this Season, praying that the gossip over my father's indiscretions had faded somewhat." A weight began to settle on her shoulders again. "Alas, it seems that they have not forgotten, for a large number of guests this evening have completely ignored our presence. Though I am grateful to Lady Jennings for her kindness, and I am grateful to all of you for being willing to speak with me."

"But of course! Whilst there is nothing very much that can be done as regards our standing, we will have each other as companions, and that is pleasant indeed."

There was a sense of contentment in Lady Frederica's voice and though Alice smiled, she felt her heavy heart sink a little lower. That was all there was to be for her, then. Yes, companionship was a great blessing, but she was not to have the one thing she had hoped for – a match.

"It does seem so very unfair, does it not?" Miss Fairley sighed and looked out across the ballroom. "There are so many gentlemen and ladies present, and yet very few of them will look in our direction."

Alice let her gaze drift across the room, noting how one young lady within a small group was speaking rapidly, her eyes flashing as the gentleman she spoke to recoiled. Wondering who the lady might be, and what had caused her to speak with such passion, Alice studied the group for a little while longer, only tugging her gaze away when the young lady's mother – or the woman Alice presumed was her mother – took her away and the conversation was ended.

"It must be difficult to be acquainted with anyone, so the chances of being asked to dance or even being conversed with are small indeed!"

"That does not mean that we do not know who *they* are." A quick grin flashed across Miss Simmons' face. "That is the way with wallflowers, Lady Alice. We stand and keep ourselves in the shadows, but our eyes see everything and take it all in. I could name almost every guest I see here and more than that, I could tell you which gentlemen are scoundrels, and which ladies are the very worst of gossips!"

Alice's eyes rounded.

"Could you truly do so?"

"I could!" Miss Simmons tilted her head, then gestured to the lady a little away from Alice in the group she had been watching previously. "That woman there is Lady Dartford. Her son is standing next to her, Lord

Dartford. She is one of the most prolific gossips in all of London, and ought to be avoided at all costs!"

"I shall remember that. No doubt she would give my mother the cut direct if they were to be acquainted!"

"Yes, I think she would do so. Her son is rather arrogant, and should be avoided also."

Miss Fairley spoke now, coming to point out one or two more guests to Alice, who found herself smiling, enjoying every moment of their conversation. Meeting these ladies had been exactly what she had needed. Listening, she took in everything each of her new acquaintances said, only for her gaze to catch on one of the most handsome gentlemen she had ever seen.

The gentleman in question wandered across the room, coming closer and closer to them, but without ever looking in their direction. His eyes flashed from one side of the room to the other, taking in everything, and yet never pausing to linger on someone or something for even a moment. His hands were clasped lightly behind his back, making his broad shoulders all the more prominent. With fair hair brushed back from his forehead and eyes which Alice was certain were blue, a strong jaw, and a gentle smile on his lips, she found herself quite lost in him.

"You are staring at Lord Sedgewick."

A quiet voice made Alice jump and she turned, blushing furiously as Miss Simmons lifted an eyebrow in her direction.

"I was not staring." When Miss Simmons laughed, Alice found herself smiling too, though her face still remained as red as could be. "Very well, I *was* staring, though I did not mean to. Lord Sedgewick, did you say?"

Miss Simmons nodded.

"A Marquess."

"Oh." Alice's heart, which had been beating a little more quickly than usual, immediately began to slow. "I see." A Marquess was a gentleman who certainly would not even look at a wallflower, even if she *was* the daughter of an Earl. "A handsome gentleman, certainly."

"Very handsome and, from what I understand, an excellent character. He is not a rogue or a scoundrel, or anything in that regard - which to my mind is rather unexpected, given that he is so high in status. Usually, gentlemen such as he are inclined to all manner of things, for they can be forgiven for almost anything due to their standing, but he, from what I have learned, is not inclined to any such behavior."

Alice's heart twisted with a sharp, sudden pain which had her catching her breath. It was not that she found the idea of Lord Sedgewick having such a high character to be troubling, more that the awareness of how different they were in standing created a gulf between them. They were not acquainted and, given what had happened with her father and the consequences thereof, were not likely to be.

I shall have to admire him from a distance. Her eyes closed tightly as a swell of tears began to push against her eyelids. *For that, I suppose, is what wallflowers are supposed to do.*

"And that gentleman there is quite the opposite of Lord Sedgewick," Miss Fairley murmured, obviously entirely unaware of all the difficulty going through Alice's heart at that moment. "Lord Cartwright is a gentleman who will pursue everything he ought not to do and will laugh about it thereafter."

"He has attempted to come to each of us at one time or another." Lady Frederica warned, her eyes narrowing a little. "He will, no doubt, come to you with a proposition most untoward. I tell you this now so that you might prepare yourself to refuse him, and so the shock will not be as great as it was for me, when he first spoke to me!" Her eyes flashed, and her jaw was tight. "He took my stunned silence as agreement, as consent, and attempted to take me from the ballroom at that very moment! I have never been so grateful for my friends as I was that evening."

"Thank you for warning me." Alice licked her lips, feeling as though she were in a great, deep pool and only just managing to keep her head above water. "Is that very common? Does it happen to wallflowers often?" Her eyes went first to Miss Fairley, then to Lady Frederica, and finally to Miss Simmons, all of whom looked back at her with a steadiness in their gaze which offered her the answer to her question without so much as a word. "Goodness. I do not quite know what to make of that."

The three ladies nodded and looked at each other, a weariness coming into each of their expressions.

"It is something that every wallflower must become used to," Lady Frederica said, eventually. "We are no longer considered as every other respectable young lady is. Instead, given that society considers us unworthy of such consideration, the only thing we are good for is the unwelcome attentions of particular gentlemen. We are there only as playthings, as distractions, and as not anything more. I have heard that, over time, some wallflowers do give in, but I am determined not to be such a lady. No matter how difficult things become, I will *never* permit any gentleman to treat me poorly."

"Nor I." With a nod to herself, Alice allowed her gaze to settle upon the handsome gentleman once more, letting a sigh escape her. "As you have said, no matter how difficult it all becomes, I will never be anything more than a proper and genteel young lady… even if I am now nothing more than a wallflower."

CHAPTER TWO

Looking back at his reflection, Simon Bellwood, Marquess of Sedgewick, smoothed one hand over his hair, even though everything was just as it ought to be. There was a strange, unsettling nervousness about the first ball of the London Season, even though there was no reason for him to feel any anxiety. He had been here many times over the years, and this Season was no different.

Though Lord Taylor is now married and will not be present as he has always been.

Last Season, his closest friend had found himself quite in love with the beautiful Lady Florentina and had quickly become betrothed. Thus far, their marriage appeared to be very contented indeed, but Simon was not about to pretend that he did not feel the loss of his friend's good company. Fully aware that he was a gentleman who preferred quiet company, and that most of his other acquaintances were rather loud and exuberant, Simon sighed quietly and wondered if he ought to have come to

London at all. Perhaps he would have been better residing at home for the Season instead of coming to Town – but the prospect of being almost entirely alone for months at a time was a little less desirable than being in London.

"The carriage is ready, my Lord."

Simon turned and nodded, making his way to the door, and murmuring his thanks to his valet. There was no more time to wait, no more moments to linger and wonder over his decision. It was time to make his way back into London society.

～

"Good evening."

Nodding and smiling, Simon continued to wander through the ballroom, finding himself still rather ill at ease. It was not as though he could not stop and converse at length with those whom he was greeting, but rather that he was choosing not to do so. Giving himself time to take in all that surrounded him – the laughter, the music, the noise, and the crush of the crowd, Simon walked slowly, his hands clasped lightly behind his back. Bit by bit, his heart lifted free of the anxiety that had twisted around it, and he found himself smiling. Even without his closest friend present, he was certain to have a very enjoyable time here in London. He simply had to avail himself of all that it offered.

Wallflowers.

Simon took them in, his gaze darting over each lady in turn. To his mind, there was a beauty in each of them that he could not easily ignore and quietly, he began to wonder what it was that each of them had done which deserved such a fate as to be sent to hide in the shadows. His gaze lingered on a young lady, her brown hair pulled up into ringlets that cascaded from the back of her head, her cream gown in sharp contrast to her dark eyes. When her eyes lifted to his, a jolt ran through him and Simon looked away quickly, a little embarrassed to have been caught studying her.

I do wonder why such a beauty has been forced to step back from the light.

Continuing his walk, he pulled his gaze and his thoughts away from the lady and the remaining wallflowers until, finally, an acquaintance pulled him into conversation.

"Lord Sedgewick!"

Turning, Simon nodded in acknowledgment of Lord Larbert, expecting to be able to continue walking, only for Lord Larbert to step out from the group he had been with, clearly eager to continue the conversation with Simon.

"Come and join us! You are quite without Lord Taylor and thus you must permit *us* to enjoy your company this Season."

Simon chuckled, despite his disinclination to join a large group for company and conversation.

"Yes, Lord Taylor is wed, but I was not only acquainted with him – I do have other acquaintances!"

"Then you must prove that." Lord Larbert chuckled, gesturing to the others who were all standing in a group together. "Come and speak with us. Tell us of your plans for this Season, should you have any!"

Still a little reluctant, but realizing that he could not spend all of his time at the ball walking around the ballroom and nodding at others, Simon went along with Lord Larbert and quickly found himself introduced to both new and old acquaintances such as Lord Hinchley, Lord Kennington, Lady Grace, and Miss Stone. The conversation moved from one topic to the next, and Simon listened carefully, adding to it when he felt able to, but otherwise allowing the conversation to flow without hindrance.

"And are you in London merely to enjoy yourself this Season, Lord Sedgewick?" Lady Elizabeth tilted her head and smiled brightly at him as Simon returned her greeting with a polite yet restrained smile of his own. "Or is there something more which you have come looking for?"

Thinking this a rather bold question and indeed, flushing hot at the curious glint in Lady Elizabeth's eye, Simon struggled to find an answer.

"I – I would say that I... I am glad to be back in London, I think."

Lady Elizabeth laughed and tossed her head.

"But that is no answer at all, Lord Sedgewick! I do wonder, now that Lord Taylor has found *his* match, if you might begin to consider your own?"

Simon looked away, his mouth going dry. Thankfully, Lady Elizabeth's question remained unanswered for a Miss Lorimer interrupted the silence by asking Lord Larbert about his thoughts as regarded the London

Season and who might be considered as a diamond of the first water – and Simon's response was no longer required. Lady Elizabeth's question, however, continued to linger in his thoughts, and though the conversation between them all carried on, he did not listen with more than half an ear.

Why was he here in London? Had he come just to enjoy the company he could find here? Simply to enjoy the dances, the laughter, and conversation? Or was he, as Lady Elizabeth had asked, seeking out a match for himself?

I have never truly considered it, though I have always known it is something I will eventually be required to do.

Frowning, Simon looked across the ballroom, his gaze going beyond the shoulders of those in his direct company. The room was filled with young, eligible ladies, but the thought of choosing only one out of them all soon became a little overwhelming. There were so many faces, so many smiles and laughing eyes, how was he meant to decide on only one?

"Who is it that you are considering?"

Simon jumped in surprise, turning to see Lord Larbert grinning at him.

"I am not considering anyone. In truth, I am thinking about what I am to do this Season."

"Do?" Lord Larbert tilted his head. "What do you mean?"

"After Lady Elizabeth's question–"

"A rather impertinent question!"

Simon grinned.

"Mayhap, yes. However, that question is something

that *has* made me think about whether or not I ought to be taking my responsibilities seriously."

"Responsibilities?"

Nodding, Simon lifted his shoulders high and let them fall again in a somewhat exaggerated shrug.

"My responsibility to marry and produce the required heir. I have not done that as yet." Lord Larbert nodded but said nothing. "It is every gentleman's responsibility, I suppose," Simon continued, wondering why Lord Larbert had not agreed with him as yet. "I must think on it at the very least, though I confess to being a little overwhelmed by the sheer number of young ladies present."

At this, Lord Larbert finally responded, a broad smile spreading right across his face and sending sparks into his eyes.

"But that presents no difficulty, surely? You simply have to make your way through society, dance with as many young ladies as you can, and acquaint yourself with even more! And then, quite unexpectedly, you will find your eyes drawn to one young lady in particular and you will know then that *she* is the one that you are interested in."

Simon shook his head and Lord Larbert's smile fell.

"I do not think that I need to be drawn in any particular way to the lady in question. I only need to know that she is suitable to my requirements."

"Suitable?" Lord Larbert lifted an eyebrow. "Surely you must desire to feel *something* for your wife?"

"I do not think so. I do not see it as relevant. Perhaps

that is why I am a little overwhelmed by the sheer amount of choice presented before me."

Lord Larbert blinked as though Simon had said something so preposterous that he could not quite take it in. Heat began to build in Simon's chest, and he cleared his throat gruffly, looking away.

"Forgive me." His acquaintance set one hand on Simon's shoulder for a moment. "I do not mean to appear so surprised, though I can tell that my reaction is apparent to you. It is only that I believed someone such as yourself would see the benefits of being drawn to one's wife, that is all."

Simon frowned.

"Someone such as myself?"

"You are someone who thinks a great deal." Lord Larbert's look of surprise melted into one of embarrassment, his face flushing as he took his eyes from Simon's. "I will admit to being a little more eager to listen to my heart, though that does not always bring about the very best of things. We have been acquainted for some time and although I am certainly not your closest friend, I am aware of your character, and how different it is from my own. You are inclined to consider all things at all times in great detail, thinking about what the consequences of any particular action might be. I would have thought, therefore, that your thoughts might have pointed you in an entirely different direction when it comes to thinking of a bride."

For whatever reason, Simon's eyes were drawn back to the wallflowers who stood apart from everyone else. In that regard, he supposed, he *had* thought about his potential bride-to-be, for even in glancing at them, he had known that he could not draw near to any of them, even if his eyes were begging him to look upon that one particular wallflower again.

He did not allow himself to do so.

"I have thought about what it would be like to marry someone entirely improper," he replied, though Lord Larbert shook his head. "That is not what you mean, then?"

"You appear to be quite contented with the idea of being wed to someone who has no affection or genuine interest in you. In that regard, I cannot agree. The consequences of such a match would, I think, be severe."

Simon snorted and rolled his eyes, drawing a look of astonishment from his friend.

"I hardly think so. My parents were not at all interested in each other and they were both very contented, in their way."

"Were they?" Lord Larbert tilted his head, and a storm began to grow in Simon's heart. "My parents were very much in love with one another and the happiness, warmth, and joy which filled our house was something I cannot help but desire for myself. That is not to say that there were not difficult times, days with more cold than warmth but, on the whole, it is something which I have decided I cannot be without."

This was something that Simon had never considered but he barely gave it a moment's thought, quite certain that his position was more than satisfactory.

"I hope that you find what you are looking for."

"You will not even think about it?"

Simon shook his head.

"It sounds to me like you will have to put in a good deal more effort, more consideration, and thought than *I* shall have to do and, in that regard, I feel myself quite contented with my decision."

Lord Larbert shrugged, his grin indicating that he was not in the least bit upset with Simon's dismissal of what he had said.

"Very well. Let us see if you still feel that way in a few weeks' time."

Another frown spread across Simon's forehead.

"What do you mean by that?"

Lord Larbert put out his hands, spreading his arms wide as he gestured to the room.

"Merely that there are so many young ladies, so much beauty and elegance all around, I think you will find it very difficult indeed to remain so sober-minded."

With a sniff, Simon lifted his chin a little, looking around the room, a hint of disregard in his gaze.

"I do not think that I will find it difficult at all," he claimed, ignoring the way that his eyes pulled to the wallflowers again. "I wager it will be very easy indeed."

"Is that so?" Lord Larbert chuckled and slapped Simon on the back. "We shall see, my friend. We shall see."

CHAPTER THREE

"And this is all that we are to do?"
"If by 'all', you mean standing at the back of the room and watching all that goes on, then yes."

Alice offered a wry smile to the new young lady who had only recently come to join them.

"It is a rather dull situation, I am afraid."

"Dull?" Miss Bosworth exclaimed, turning to shoot a sharp gaze at Alice as though she were somehow responsible for her current change in circumstances. "It is more than dull! I am not about to become a staid, gray creature who clings to the shadows and never once steps out into the light."

"I am afraid that is what is expected of us."

"And why should we do what society expects?"

It was a question which Alice had not thought about before. It was now a fortnight since she had come to London, a fortnight since she had realized that she was best suited to hiding with the other wallflowers, and a fortnight since she had felt herself lose hope.

Miss Bosworth had not yet reached that understanding. She was upset – and understandably so – but it did not mean that she was able to continue as she was used to. Instead, she was going to have to become used to the idea of staying back from the other guests, of keeping herself hidden until, mayhap, a lady or a gentleman might take notice of her for even a short while.

It was not pleasant, but what choice did Alice and the other wallflowers have but to accept it?

"You have not answered my question, Lady Alice."

There was no challenge nor unkindness in the lady's voice, but her eyes were sharp as she arched one eyebrow.

"I can give you no answer," Alice replied, quietly.

Miss Bosworth sighed and looked away, beginning to strike up a conversation with another of the ladies, leaving Alice to look out across the room. The ball was going wonderfully well for those who were able to enjoy it and, try as she might to find a little happiness within her heart, there was nothing there but sorrow. How much she wished that *she* could step out to dance, that gentlemen would be signing *her* dance card just as they had done last Season, before news of her father's wrongdoings had spread through society. Heaving a sigh, she blinked away a flurry of tears, refusing to let a single one fall. It was the unfairness of it all that upset her the most. After all, she had done nothing deserving of such treatment and yet *she* was the one being punished for her father's wrongdoings.

It was all so very upsetting.

"We must do *something*."

A little surprised, Alice looked to see Miss Bosworth

gesturing to them all, her face suddenly alive with a new energy that Alice could not quite understand. What happiness was there in being a wallflower?

"Listen to me, all of you," Miss Bosworth continued, as the other wallflowers came to stand a little closer to her. "Here we are, all standing here at the back of the ballroom without hope of stepping out to dance, without the expectation of good company or the like – and for what reason? None of us have done anything worthy of condemnation. We have been pushed aside by society, but that does not mean that we have to remain as we are."

It was the very same discussion they had shared only a few moments ago, and Alice frowned, wondering why it was that Miss Bosworth continued to speak in such a way. Could she not accept her position as a wallflower?

"I do not understand what you mean. We are wallflowers. What more can we expect?"

Miss Bosworth smiled, but her gaze grew stern.

"We do not have to do as society expects of us, as I have only just said to you. The *ton* believes that wallflowers must stand at the back of the room, silent and unimposing. I say that we do *not* have to do as they demand. Instead, we might walk, two or three together, about the ballroom, in amongst the guests, and seek to be seen and to be noticed. It might not change a great deal about our situation, but it will make us feel more significant, will it not? It will make certain that we are not forgotten! Even if society thinks that we ought not to do anything akin to such a thing, why should it matter? We are already wallflowers. Do we truly wish to act as they demand? Do we wish to shrink back, to hide ourselves away, and sink into the darkness?"

A furious burst of hope flew through Alice's form and sent a flash of light into her eyes. Was Miss Bosworth correct? Was there a way for them not to stand back, not to hide away as was expected?

What could happen if we were to step out? Her heart began to thud as she slowly began to nod, seeing Miss Simmons begin to smile. *The ton could not censure us more than it has already done, surely?*

"We could stand together and converse as so many others do." Speaking with an obvious excitement ringing through her voice, Miss Simmons' eyes flared. "We do not have to hide here, do we? We could stand in amongst the other guests and talk together, even if no one else wishes to talk to us. What could be wrong with that?"

Alice found herself nodding in agreement. Miss Simmons was quite right, there was nothing improper about talking together, was there?

"There is *nothing* wrong with that," Miss Bosworth declared, her eyes like steel. "It will take courage, certainly, but I, for one, am quite determined to step out and behave just as I please. Society might continue to call me a wallflower, but I will not behave as one."

But will I?

Alice bit her lip and then looked to the floor, her breathing quickening. Her friends murmured and whispered together but Alice let herself think without any interruption, listening to her own thoughts and wondering whether it would be a wise course of action. Yes, she was eager to return to society, eager to make her way back to what she had once known, but that was most unlikely, given the disgrace surrounding her father. Therefore, could she not do *something*, anything, to make herself a little bit more present within society? It might give her a little more hope, and that had to be a good thing for, at the present moment, she had no hope whatsoever and felt herself fading away.

Yes. I can do this.

"I do not know what my mother would think." Miss Simmons looked at Alice, her worries suddenly evident. "I fear what she would think."

"I can understand that." Alice smiled gently and squeezed her friend's hand. "But I think that we must consider what it would be like if we remained here rather than risking our parents' upset."

Miss Bosworth nodded her agreement.

"My mother might also have something to say on the matter. But if I walk with my friends through the ballroom, then I am not alone, I am not without company. There can be nothing said against that in terms of propriety."

Miss Simmons nodded slowly, though she did not immediately appear enthusiastic.

"That is true."

"It is *very* true," Alice whispered, as Lady Frederica spoke of her concerns.

"Come, my dear friend. Let us be brave. What is better? To stay here, hiding away, pushed aside and ignored? Or to be bold and to step out into the center of the room with the other guests, forcing them to take note of us?"

Miss Simmons let out a slow breath and nodded, though her eyes closed for a moment as if she were fighting to find the courage she needed.

"I will be with you," Alice promised, fighting back her own nervousness which urged her to stay where she was, to step back into the shadows which had become so familiar and safe over the last two weeks. "Who knows? Mayhap a gentleman will take notice of us!"

Miss Simmons' eyes flared.

"But we are wallflowers?" What will they care for that?"

"It is impossible to tell what might happen." With a smile, Alice leaned closer to her friend. "Not every gentleman will ignore us, I am sure of it. We may even get to dance!" Her friend caught her breath and Alice laughed, her fears vanishing completely. "We can have hope of these things *if* we are bold and step out," Alice continued, as Miss Simmons slowly began to smile. "But if we stay here, as we are expected to do, we have no hope at all."

"I – I think I can do it." Miss Simmons' smile was a little uncertain and she looked over to the others. "What of the rest of you?"

Miss Bosworth and Lady Frederica were already arm in arm.

"It is entirely up to you," Miss Bosworth said quietly. "Though Lady Frederica and I are to step out. Would anyone else wish to join us?"

With a nod, Alice moved to take Miss Bosworth's other arm, smiling her encouragement to Miss Simmons. It only took a few moments, but it was with great relief that not only Miss Simmons, but Miss Fairley also agreed to walk out together. Alice held her head high as she, Miss Bosworth, and Lady Frederica began their promenade around the room, keeping her gaze fixed straight ahead and ignoring the looks from the other guests which she was certain were turned in her direction. With growing confidence, she pinned a smile to her face and walked through the ballroom, just as she had done on her very first Season here in London.

It was the most wonderful, freeing sensation and, for the first time in many days, Alice finally found that her heart open and hopeful again. Perhaps there was a chance for her to find a little happiness in this Season after all.

∼

Heat ran up from Alice's core as her breath hitched, merely from the simple act of letting her eyes linger on one particular gentleman. The very same gentleman who had caught her attention some time ago, when her friends had been busy pointing out the different gentlemen and ladies to her.

Lord Sedgewick.

The way that his eyes roved around the room caught her interest and she found herself gazing at him, wondering what it was that he was thinking, and why he continued to look at the assembled company rather than engaging himself in conversation with the other gentlemen and ladies he stood with. What was he thinking? Was he looking for someone?

Her smile tipped a little ruefully. *He certainly will not be looking for a wallflower.*

Without warning, the gentleman's gaze turned to her and, given that she was already staring at him, their eyes met and Alice gasped, a hiccupping breath tight in her throat. Lord Sedgewick did not look elsewhere, did not pull his gaze away, but continued to look at her as though she were the very object he had been searching for.

"Lord Sedgewick is looking at you."

Alice glanced at Lady Frederica, but when she looked back to Lord Sedgewick, he was no longer gazing at her.

"He was, yes."

"You are not acquainted with him as yet, though?"

"No, I am not."

Lady Frederica smiled.

"I am. It was before I was forced to become a wallflower, however. I thought him a quiet sort."

"Quiet?"

Her friend nodded.

"Quiet and considered in everything."

Alice thought about this for a few moments, then smiled.

"I think that such traits are preferable to having a gentleman who is overly loud and ill-considered."

Lady Frederica laughed.

"Certainly, I would agree." Her smile grew bigger. "I must say, it is almost a relief to be able to stand amongst the other guests and laugh and smile so, even if it *is* with each other. I–"

"Lady Frederica. Good evening."

Alice jumped in surprise at the unexpected voice that came from over her shoulder, turning to see none other than Lord Sedgewick bowing toward Lady Frederica. Her heart began to beat furiously as she took a small step back, a little worried that somehow, he would know that they had been discussing him, even though the thought was foolish indeed.

"Lord Sedgewick, good evening. How very kind of you to greet us."

"Of course." Clearing his throat, Lord Sedgewick turned his eyes to Alice who, blushing, looked quickly to Lady Frederica, silently begging her to make the appropriate introduction.

"Might I present my new acquaintance and my friend, Lady Alice, daughter to the Earl of Talbot?" Lady Frederica spoke with an ease that had Alice's heart slowing just a little. "Lady Alice, this is the Marquess of Sedgewick."

"Very pleased to make your acquaintance, Lady Alice." Lord Sedgewick bowed toward her and then lifted his head, just as Alice finished her curtsey. "I had noted you in company with Lady Frederica."

Alice blinked.

"Oh. Well, yes, we are newly acquainted this Season, but we have fast become dear friends. I–"

"Lord Sedgewick, whatever *are* you doing?" The words overrode her own, and Alice stuttered to a stop just as the young lady who had spoken laughingly pulled at Lord Sedgewick's arm, another young lady beside her. "You must not speak with these two ladies, not when there is much better company to be had!"

The sharpness of Lord Sedgewick's look had Alice's face burning, though she did not pull her gaze away from his. Instead, she kept it steady but did not say a word, wishing that she dared to speak back to this young lady who had been so very rude in her manner and in her words.

"Is there something the matter?"

Lord Sedgewick looked first at Alice and then back to the young lady who, laughing, curled her hand around his arm all the more.

"Of course there is!" she exclaimed.

Alice coughed lightly, in the hope of reminding the young lady that she was being very rude indeed but, as she had expected, the young lady herself simply ignored her. It was as if she was not even there. A glance at Lady Frederica told Alice that her friend was both upset and embarrassed, given the red spots in her cheeks and the slight narrowing of her eyes, but again, she also said nothing.

"There is nothing the matter." Alice found herself speaking quickly, bringing the young lady's attention directly to her. "Lady Frederica was making the introductions before you so *rudely* interrupted, that is all."

The young woman tossed her head but did not release Lord Sedgewick's arm.

"You are both wallflowers," she said, dismissively. "Come now, Lord Sedgewick, come and speak with those who are of equal standing. These wallflowers need not be considered."

Alice closed her eyes against a wave of anger and sadness which combined to threaten to overwhelm her entirely. Taking a long breath, she opened her eyes again, ready to speak to Lord Sedgewick and to this young lady but, much to her disappointment, Lord Sedgewick was already walking away.

"What... what happened?"

Lady Frederica sighed and shook her head.

"I believe that we have just discovered that Lord Sedgewick is unwilling to be seen with a wallflower," she answered, quietly. "That is discouraging. I had hoped that he would have been a gentleman with a little more consideration."

Alice swallowed hard, more disheartened than she could say. For whatever reason, her attention had been drawn to Lord Sedgewick and now, much to her chagrin, he had proven himself to be as unwilling as any other guest to even *think* of spending a prolonged time in her company. With a heavy heart, she turned away and walked back towards the edge of the ballroom, leaving Lady Frederica behind. At that moment, all she wanted was to be in amongst the shadows, to step back into the darkness and hide away until this ball and all its disappointments came to an end.

CHAPTER FOUR

"Wallflowers."

Simon frowned and looked at Lord Larbert.

"What of them?"

"I heard that Lady Clara took you from the company of two of them," Lord Larbert answered as they both walked down the street, passing various shops and other establishments as they went. "It was good of you to go with her – with Lady Elizabeth, I mean. To stay in prolonged conversation with wallflowers is unwise."

Saying nothing, Simon looked away, aware of the guilt that stabbed through him at his friend's remarks. The truth was, he had been thinking of his actions from two nights ago, and was not certain that he had made the right choice. He had been previously acquainted with Lady Frederica, and it had seemed churlish to walk away from her, simply because she was now a wallflower.

And yet, he had done so all the same, simply because Lady Clara – a new acquaintance – had asked him to.

That was not the right thing to have done, he was sure of that. He ought to have listened to his own heart and made his own judgments rather than continue as Lady Clara had asked of him.

Thus far, the young ladies I have met are all much too sure of themselves and far too demanding.

"That is not true," Lord Larbert snorted, making Simon realize that he had spoken aloud. "You are only speaking of Lady Elizabeth and Lady Clara, I am sure, and while I will agree that they are both very confident young ladies who speak their minds without a great deal of consideration, they have a great many other attributes which lift them up very well, I think."

"Oh?" Simon lifted an eyebrow. "And what might those be?"

Lord Larbert chuckled, and Simon grinned, glad that he had managed to move the conversation away from himself and back towards his friend instead.

"Lady Elizabeth is *very* beautiful, and Lady Clara has the most elegant figure." Speaking quite candidly, Lord Larbert laughed again when Simon threw him a look. "Do not think that I intend to seek either of them out for myself, however, for I certainly have no intention of doing anything like that. Yes, they are both fair of face, but I am not inclined towards either one of them, not in that way. Though you might think of them?"

Simon shook his head no.

"But why not?" his friend persisted, as Simon began to scowl. "They are eligible, genteel young ladies and that is precisely what you are looking for, is it not?"

Simon opened his mouth to give a reason as to why he could not consider either of the young ladies, only to close it again. Seeing his friend about to burst into triumphant laughter, Simon held up one hand, a thought coming to him.

"I do not consider them because Lady Elizabeth is a little too impolite for my tastes and Lady Clara is thoughtless."

The laughter in Lord Larbert's face quickly faded.

"Impolite? Thoughtless? In what way?"

"Do you recall the questions she flung at me when we were first acquainted? I could hardly believe she had the audacity to ask me such a thing as that."

Slowly beginning to nod, Lord Larbert rubbed his chin.

"Yes, I suppose that is fair."

"And Lady Clara spoke in a manner I did not like towards the two wallflowers, though I confess that I must also hold myself responsible, for I did go with her when she requested it."

Seeing Lord Larbert's questioning look, Simon quickly explained, only for Lord Larbert to shrug.

"They are wallflowers," he said, as though this explained everything. "You cannot expect them to be treated in the same way as every other young lady. It would damage your reputation to be seen in their company very often."

A curl of distaste rose in Simon's stomach, and he shook his head.

"I do not agree with that. Unless, of course, there is good reason for them to be considered wallflowers? I was surprised to see Lady Frederica there. I was well acquainted with her family not two Seasons ago."

"Her sister… there was a scandal." Lord Larbert spread his hands. "Such disgrace, it touches every family member and thus, Lady Frederica is no longer considered a worthy member of society."

Simon grimaced.

"It seems rather unfair, but I suppose that is how society works." Tilting his head and praying that his friend did not see any change in his expression, he continued. "There was a Lady Alice there also. Have you heard of her?"

Lord Larbert shook his head.

"No, I am not acquainted with her. Who is her family?"

"Lord Talbot. An Earl, from what I remember."

In an instant, Lord Larbert's eyes flared, and Simon's stomach dropped.

"Oh yes, I recall Lord Talbot. Why, that was only last year! I am surprised that the young lady thought to come to London – or that her father thought to bring her!"

"Lord Talbot is not present. Lady Talbot is the one who brought Lady Alice to the Season."

His friend shook his head and sighed.

"It is another example of a family disgrace which, even though Lady Alice must surely be an amiable, intelligent, and genteel young lady, will render her less than suitable."

Simon swallowed, wondering whether he truly wished to know what it was that Lord Talbot had done, but found the questions coming to his lips regardless.

"It must have been a deep disgrace, then?"

Lord Larbert nodded.

"It was revealed last Season that Lord Talbot not only frequented brothels on a regular basis, but he was also deep in debt to them *and* to various gentlemen against whom he had played cards – and lost. He had refused to pay and thus, one of them decided to make his actions known to all and sundry. The scandal was severe, and Lord Talbot took his daughter and his wife back to his estate very soon thereafter."

Simon's eyes widened.

"Goodness. And Lady Talbot dared to bring her daughter back to London for *this* Season? I am surprised. Surely, she would have been able to perceive that the *ton* would turn their back on her?"

"I would presume so... but perhaps she thought it was worth it. Mayhap a less fortunate gentleman, one with a lower standing than others for some reason; that sort of gentleman might approach her daughter, the scandal notwithstanding. That could be her reasoning." The thought of Lady Alice marrying a Baron, or some poor, degenerate gentleman, simply so that she might call herself a married woman was, to Simon's mind, a most unbecoming situation. Though he understood the reasons for a lady being forced to stand as a wallflower, it still displeased him greatly. Shaking his head to himself, he caught Lord Larbert's eye but said nothing more, choosing to set the entire matter aside. "Look, now," Lord Larbert said, indicating a group of young ladies standing together by the milliner's shop. "*These* are some of the ladies whom we ought to be considering. Let us talk no more about wallflowers and their situation. The only thing we ought to be considering is just how many *new* acquaintances we can introduce ourselves to – and how many young ladies will be known to us thereafter!"

The grin on his face made Simon chuckle and, pushing all thoughts of Lady Alice out of his mind, he followed Lord Larbert, ready to make new acquaintances.

~

"Might you be dancing this evening?" Simon kept his smile broad as he nodded first to Lady Christina and then threw a glance to her mother, who nodded fervently. "I should be very glad to step out with you."

"But of course!"

Lady Christina handed her dance card to him with a soft smile across her lips and Simon smiled at her in return, before dropping his gaze to the dance card. Her dance card was practically empty, and Simon quickly wrote down his name for the waltz, thinking that it would be best to make certain that he already had the waltz secured. Lady Christina was just the same as every other young lady he had met thus far but, all the same, Simon was determined to have every dance filled. After all, how was he to find a young lady suitable for marriage if he did not dance with any?

"Lady Christina?"

Simon looked up in surprise, having just handed the dance card back to Lady Christina.

"You are dancing, yes?"

The gentleman in question was looking only at Lady Christina and ignored Simon completely, his eyes rounded and fixed on the lady.

"Lord Steelforth, good evening." Lady Christina looked at Simon and then back to Lord Steelforth. "Forgive me, I was just speaking to Lord Sedgewick and–"

"You have not yet given *me* your dance card."

A little taken aback by the gentleman's forthright manner *and* the way that he spoke to Lady Christina, Simon cleared his throat and finally caught the gentleman's attention.

"As Lady Christina has said, she was only just speaking with me and I have, just now, returned her dance card to her. Do excuse me." Smiling at Lady Christina, he inclined his head. "I look forward to our waltz."

"The waltz?" Lord Steelforth exclaimed, throwing up one hand. "You permitted him to take the waltz?"

Simon frowned.

"I do not think that Lady Christina is obliged to give her waltz to anyone in particular, Lord Steelforth. You do her a disservice by appearing so frustrated. Permit the lady to do as she pleases and to let other gentlemen, such as myself, do as *they* please by taking whatever dance they want without interruption."

"That was meant to be mine." The anger in Lord Steelforth's voice surprised Simon, and he lifted an eyebrow, only for the gentleman to scowl all the darker. "You ought not to have taken it."

"You should have been by Lady Christina's side more promptly should you have hoped to ensure that you might gain one particular dance," Simon replied, quickly. "Now, if you will excuse me."

So saying, he turned around and began to walk away, thinking it best to leave Lady Christina and Lord Steelforth to their conversation. Whether it was that Lord Steelforth was interested in furthering his acquaintance with the lady, he could not say, but all the same, the gentleman's manner was most rude.

"Whatever was that?"

Simon rolled his eyes as Lord Larbert came to join him.

"That was Lord Steelforth practically demanding that I return the waltz I had taken to Lady Christina's dance card so that *he* might have it."

Lord Larbert's eyebrows rose.

"That is strange indeed."

"It is not altogether strange," came another voice as Simon glanced to Lord Larbert's other side to see Lord Kennington joining in the conversation. "You are speaking of Lord Steelforth, yes? He is quite taken with Lady Christina, I think."

Shrugging, Simon let the remark pass right over him.

"Then he should have made his way to her side just as soon as he could so that he could have the dance he wished for."

"That is a little harsh," came the mild reply as Lord Kennington threw him a quick glance. "The gentleman might have only just arrived, and this was as quickly as he could make it into the ballroom. He is about to ask to court the lady, I believe."

"If he has settled on her, then he should so at once –

but neither should he care if another gentleman takes the waltz from the lady. It is not as though I am interested in furthering my acquaintance with her."

Lord Kennington frowned and even Lord Larbert let out an exclamation of surprise.

"Why would you dance with her, then, if you had no real interest in the lady?"

Simon shrugged.

"I must acquaint myself with as many young ladies as I can so that I know which of them I might consider. If Lady Christina already has interest from another gentleman, then why should I step in the way of that?"

"Because you might have an affection for her?" Lord Kennington slowed his steps and turned so that he might face Simon directly, bringing him to a stop also. "Is that so very surprising?"

"That I should have an affection for the lady?" Simon considered this, tilting his head a little. "I have already said to Lord Larbert that such things are not what I require for myself. I do not think that I want to have any sort of emotional intimacy with the lady I marry and thus, I do not require either the lady or myself to have any *feelings*."

Lord Larbert nudged Lord Kennington, rolling his eyes as he did so.

"I have attempted to remove this idea from him, but he ignores me outright."

"There is nothing wrong with that!" Simon protested, only to hear an exclamation coming from one side of the ballroom.

Turning his head, his eyes flew wide at the sight of a

gentleman leaning over a young lady though, given the dark shadows at the side of the ballroom, he could not quite make out who it was. The gentleman in question was laughing, one hand wrapped around the lady's wrist and pressing her back against the wall.

It is one of the wallflowers.

"Look, there." Lifting his chin, he gestured to the wallflower and the gentleman, with both Lord Larbert and Lord Kennington turning to look. "We should intervene."

Lord Kennington snorted.

"It is only Lord Cartwright. He will do whatever he can for a little bit of pleasure."

"Except the young lady does not look as though she wishes for his attentions."

Simon's heart began to pound as the young lady recoiled, twisting her head away from Lord Cartwright's advances. Wallflower or not, she did not deserve to be treated in such a way and, without thought as to his own reputation or what his friends might think of him, Simon strode directly across the room towards them and, with his blood roaring fire into his veins, pulled Lord Cartwright back from the young lady and, when the gentleman lurched back towards him in a rage, promptly planted one fist into the side of the man's face.

CHAPTER FIVE

I hope that they are enjoying themselves.

Alice sighed quietly and dropped her head forward, squeezing her eyes closed. The other wallflowers were not at this particular ball. They and their parents had all been invited to a soiree and given that there would be fewer guests, they might have more opportunity to be noticed by others. Tonight, however, Alice recognized that she had nothing to do other than stand at the side of the ballroom and silently hope that someone might be kind enough to talk to her. Her mother had thought to stay with her, but Alice had urged her to go and find her own friends, not wishing her to stand at the back of the room as she did, sinking into the shadows until she felt as though she were one of them.

"You ought not to be standing here alone."

Alice turned her head and jumped in surprise, astonished when a gentleman appeared to step out of the gloom and lingered near to her.

"I am quite all right."

Turning her head back, she kept her gaze away from him and prayed that he would understand that she did not want to have anything more to do with his company.

The gentleman did not take notice.

"I should have thought that a beautiful young lady like you should be out dancing and conversing with all of your acquaintances," the gentleman said, running one finger down Alice's bare arm and making her recoil, stepping away from him and wishing that she was not so close to the wall – and so far from her mother. "But then I discovered who you were *and* who your father is, and everything made sense."

"*I* have done nothing wrong," Alice shot back, hearing the disdain in his words, and looking back at him sharply. "Forgive me, sir, but, given that we are not acquainted, I do not feel able to continue this conversation. Good evening."

"Ah, but you are a wallflower and thus, your demands and requirements are not the same as those of every other young lady."

Far from listening to her desire for him to step away, the gentleman came closer and this time, caught her hand in his. Alice tried to pull it away, her heart beginning to pound furiously in her chest, but the gentleman would not permit her to leave. Rather than cry out, she let her hand go limp, still praying silently that either he would take his leave or that her mother would return and see what he was attempting to do. A quick glance around told her that she had only a few other guests near her and none had even glanced in her direction. She did not think, therefore, that there was to be any help offered her... which meant that she would have to find a way to escape from him herself.

"You may believe that, sir, but my requirements are precisely as any other young lady's are," she hissed back, trying to dampen down her anger and take control of the situation as best she could. "I do not expect to be coerced into introductions or the like. I would prefer that, if you wish to continue speaking with me, you find someone to make the correct introductions."

"I shall make them myself," came the reply, a dark smile spreading across his face, matching the shadows in his eyes and the dark hair sweeping across his forehead. "You are already known to me and I, therefore, must make myself known to you. I am Lord Cartwright."

Lord Cartwright.

The warnings her friends had offered her at the very start of the Season came back to her and with that recollection, Alice's fear redoubled itself. Lord Cartwright would do whatever he wished to get her attentions – offered freely or otherwise – and she had no one to stand with her, no one to aid her.

What was she going to do?

"I have no interest in being in your company," she said, as clearly as she could, as her heart continued to pound. "Please, take your leave of me."

"But why should you say such a wounding thing as that?" Lord Cartwright exclaimed, moving so that he now faced her, his body so close to hers that she could feel the heat coming from it. "I have done nothing wrong. I have not injured you or insulted you. In fact, I think that you ought to be as pleased as could be that a gentleman such as myself, of such high standing and title, has come to speak with you in such a... personal manner."

At this, he moved closer, and Alice let out a cry, unable to keep hold of her fear any longer. Lord Cartwright only laughed and wrapped his arms around her waist and pulled her close against him – and Alice's heart began to beat in a furious, wild panic. She began to push and twist, trying to pull herself away from him, but Lord Cartwright had her pressed between himself and the wall, and there seemed to be very little way to escape. His head was lowering, his mouth seeking hers, and Alice let out another cry. Tears sprang to her eyes, her mouth going dry, a scream lodged in her throat – and then everything blurred before her eyes. Someone dragged Lord Cartwright back, the weight against her body was pulled away and there was no longer a scream on her lips but rather, a shout of rage from Lord Cartwright filled the air around her.

"Whatever do you think you are doing?" A loud voice roared, pulling Lord Cartwright further away. "This is not the place for this – and *she* is not the lady for it either!"

Her head spinning, Alice took a deep breath and pressed herself back against the wall in an attempt to regain her strength. Whoever this was, there was someone who came to her defense, and she could not have been more grateful. Breathing raggedly, she closed her eyes, barely hearing the conversation between the two men.

"How dare you put your hands on me?" Lord

Cartwright exclaimed, "she is nothing but a wallflower! What care you for such things?"

Alice blinked rapidly, pushing herself away from the wall as other gentlemen came closer, with some blocking her from the sight of the other guests. Shrinking back, she looked to see Lord Cartwright rubbing at his jaw, his eyes spitting fire as none other than Lord Sedgewick stood tall, though his hands were curled tight by his sides.

"You will stay away from her – and from all the other wallflowers," Lord Sedgewick returned, his tone brooking no argument from Lord Cartwright. "You are a disgrace."

The other gentlemen murmured their agreement – though none save for Lord Sedgewick had spoken to Lord Cartwright, and Alice watched Lord Cartwright's gaze slowly slide towards her and then back towards Lord Sedgewick. An ugly darkness flooded his expression, his jaw tightening, his face still red from where Lord Sedgewick had punched him.

"You have something with her already? Then why did you not say so?"

Shame burned through her and Alice dropped her head, face flaming.

"I have no connection to this young lady," she heard Lord Sedgewick say, firmly. "However, what I *do* have is respectability. I will not permit any gentleman to stand and behave in such a way towards *any* young lady when their advances are not wanted, regardless of their social standing." Lifting his chin, he stood a little taller. "I am not the sort of gentleman who would take advantage, Cartwright. I stand against such things, whilst you seek them out! Therefore, Lord Cartwright, I will stand against *you*, if I have to."

Lord Cartwright rubbed at his chin, his eyes still flashing though, much to Alice's relief, he did not make a single attempt to even step closer.

"*You* are the fool," he hissed, glaring at Lord Sedgewick. "She is a wallflower, nothing more. You could take as much advantage as you please and no one would so much as bat an eye."

"I do not think that it is foolish to stand up for the protection of young ladies, Cartwright." This time, it was not Lord Sedgewick who spoke, but another gentleman, one who looked lazily at Lord Cartwright and shrugged lightly as he spoke. "In fact, I should say that it is what ought to be expected of a gentleman. You will find no friends here, Cartwright. Not when you choose to behave like this."

Lord Cartwright's gaze narrowed, he made to say something more, and then, with a loud exclamation, turned away and strode off through the crowd.

Alice let out a breath of relief and slumped back against the wall, the meager strength she had built up within herself shattering in an instant.

"I am sorry."

Looking up, her eyes settled on Lord Sedgewick's blue ones, seeing how they flickered across her features.

"You have no need to apologize, Lord Sedgewick. Thank you for what you did."

"I apologize for the fact that I did not come over more quickly," he said in response, "and though it is not my responsibility, I should like to apologize on Lord

Cartwright's behalf also. It would be my hope that he would speak to you himself, but I highly doubt that he will do so."

Managing a small smile, Alice nodded and looked at the other gentleman who was standing nearby.

"Thank you both for speaking to him. I do not know what would have happened had you not come to intervene."

"Not at all." The second gentleman inclined his head and put one hand to his heart. "Lord Larbert. And you, I hear, are Lady Alice."

"I am."

"I confess that I would not have done a single thing unless Lord Sedgewick had not stepped out first," he told her, surprising her with his honesty. "You have Lord Sedgewick to thank for all of it. He was the one who saw your distress and decided to act upon it."

Alice swallowed hard, grateful for Lord Sedgewick's actions but, hearing Lord Larbert's honesty, hearing that he would have abandoned her to Lord Cartwright's actions, left her with a painful heart.

"Then I am all the more grateful to you, Lord Sedgewick. I am grateful that you see me just as any other young lady rather than one who does not require respect, or your aid." Her voice trembled and she closed her eyes, aware that the shock of what had occurred was still running wildly through her. "I dare not think what would have happened had you not stepped in."

"It is best not to think on it," he said, quietly, and as she opened her eyes, he reached to take her hand. The touch made her tremble, but not with fear. Instead, it was with an awareness of his nearness and of how differently she felt when she looked into his eyes. "Please, do come and speak with me, should you ever have even a hint of such difficulties again – not only from Lord Cartwright, but from any others." Bowing over her hand, he smiled when he lifted his head, a fresh warmth in his eyes that swept right through her. "Though I must hope that after what took place today, there will be no requirement for such an action again! I am certain that news of it will spread around London, and you will be all the more protected."

Alice managed a quiet laugh, though her hand was burning from where his fingers clasped hers. The relief that had come from Lord Cartwright being pulled away from her was now slowly being replaced with something else, something which she could neither identify nor understand.

"I do hope that your hand is quite all right, Lord Sedgewick. You did not need to injure yourself on my behalf."

"I would have done so for any young lady – and I would do so again. Good evening, Lady Alice."

Swallowing hard, she managed to mumble a farewell, and then watched him walk away, unable to take her eyes from him. He stood tall, walking through the other guests, seemingly oblivious to the many gazes fixed upon him. No doubt news of what he had done would be spreading through the ballroom already, but Alice did not find herself with even the smallest bit of concern. He had saved her. He had taken Lord Cartwright away and had flung him so far back that Alice knew that he would never even dream of approaching her again. Out of every gentleman and lady here, Lord Sedgewick had been the one to step forward, to take himself to her and stand up against the wrong being done. Her gratitude was more than she could even think to express... and her heart already begging her to find a way to spend even a little more time in his company.

CHAPTER SIX

"Everyone is talking about what you did."

Simon rolled his eyes.

"What they *should* be talking about is what Lord Cartwright did rather than my actions – which were taken only because of *his* dark deeds in the first place."

"All the same," Lord Larbert replied, with a shrug, "you are being spoken of throughout London. Lord Cartwright is making you out to be the very worst of gentlemen, of course, but you will be relieved to know that very few people believe him."

Shrugging, Simon let out a long sigh and let his gaze rove around the ballroom. Thus far, he had attended a dinner, a soiree, and now this ball, and, the more he stepped out, the more the whispers seemed to grow in intensity. He had tried to ignore it, but the sidelong glances and the murmurs that followed him were difficult to disregard. His thoughts had been taken up with Lady Alice, though those were also thoughts he had attempted to push away from himself - without too much success. In thinking about her, he had wondered how she had fared after the encounter with Lord Cartwright, whether she had recovered from her fright, and then why he had not seen her out in society since. Yes, she was a wallflower, but he had seen her in society fairly regularly until now, although always at the back of the room.

Which means I must have been aware of her, even though I did not recognize that until now.

"Lord Sedgewick?"

Simon cleared his throat and looked away.

"Apologies."

"You were wondering, no doubt, whether this would do any good to your reputation or if it would damage it." Lord Larbert shrugged, then grinned. "I think it will have done you some good, my friend. Every young lady will think highly of you, and none will listen to Lord Cartwright. I can assure you of that."

"Then that is a relief," Simon agreed, quickly, glad that his friend had not pressed him to know exactly what it was he had been thinking.

"It has done my reputation no good, however," Lord Larbert continued, a frown marring his expression. "I should have stepped forward a good deal more quickly than I did. I am quite ashamed of myself, for pushing aside Lord Cartwright's behavior as nothing of importance, given that the lady was only a wallflower. I ought not to have done so."

Turning to look at his friend, Simon arched an eyebrow and Lord Larbert flushed, looking away.

"Seeing Lady Alice so shaken and pale made me realize just how dreadful a situation she was in." Closing his eyes, Lord Larbert shook his head, his jaw tight. "It was not right for me to stand aside. I am grateful for your determination to step forward into a dark situation. I shall do so again myself should there be a next time."

"Then that is a good thing." Simon looked back around the room and then smiled. "Perhaps I should take advantage of the sudden interest society now has in me, and go in search of as many new acquaintances as I can."

Lord Larbert chuckled, his severe expression breaking apart quickly.

"You are still searching for a young lady who might be more suitable for you than any other, rather than one you are drawn to?"

In an instant, a vision of Lady Alice came into his mind, and try as he might, Simon could not remove it from his thoughts. Clearing his throat, he shrugged off his friend's remark and looked away, only for his gaze to settle upon the very young lady he had been thinking of.

His heart lurched.

Lady Alice was speaking to someone whom Simon presumed to be her mother, her chin lifted, her eyes sharp but still glistening. Had she been crying? Unable to take his eyes from her, Simon watched as she settled a hand on her mother's arm, nodding and smiling, and then gesturing for her mother to step away. With obvious reluctance, given the slowness of her steps and the many glances over her shoulder, the lady stepped away and Lady Alice moved back to lean against the wall of the ballroom, the smile still lingering on her lips.

The very moment that her mother reached some other ladies, that smile faded, and Lady Alice dropped her head, her hands falling loose by her sides. There came a heaviness into her shoulders, seeming to push her down into the floor, and Simon's frown grew. The urge to go to her, to speak to her, and to see the light return to her eyes was almost overwhelming, to the point that he took a step forward, only to see Lord Larbert watching him with curiosity burning in his eyes.

Simon stopped dead.

"Should you wish to join me?"

With another look around the room, his eyes flickered again to Lord Larbert who merely grinned. Did he know what Simon was thinking? Who he was considering? Despite his attempts to keep his expression quite nonchalant, he felt a slow heat begin to rise, growing from his chest and spreading up into his face. Not wishing to have his friend be at all aware of what else was going on at present, he shrugged, smiled, and stepped away, leaving Lord Larbert to decide whether to join him or not.

Forcing his steps elsewhere, moving directly away from Lady Alice, Simon made himself remember that the only young women he would be considering were suitable young ladies... and a wallflower certainly was not at all suitable for someone such as him! He had already garnered more interest by what he had done and that, certainly, was to be considered a positive change given that more young ladies and their mothers might consider him, but should he step forward into further conversation with a wallflower, then he certainly would *not* be considered in the same light. Her presence might very well damage his reputation.

"Good evening, Lady Helen." Bowing, he smiled as

the young lady dropped into a curtsey, his voice having pulled her away from the company of her mother. "Are you to dance this evening?"

"Good evening, Lord Sedgewick. Yes, I should be very glad to dance."

"Excellent."

Simon took her dance card and wrote his name down for the polka. Thereafter, he spent the next hour or so making his way around the room, signing his name to various dance cards and smiling so much that his jaw soon became rather sore.

And all the while, he thought of Lady Alice.

"The waltz."

Murmuring to himself, Simon looked about the room, wondering which other young lady he might dance with. There were a good many of them he had not spoken to as yet but, all the same, his thoughts continually returned to Lady Alice. With a sigh, he looked across the room towards her again, only for a hand to tap his shoulder.

"Are you to dance with Lady Helen?"

Simon nodded, a little surprised at Lord Westerly's dark expression.

"Yes, I am. Good evening, Lord Westerly." He tilted his head as the gentleman's frown only grew deeper. "Is there something the matter?"

"Stay away from her."

Simon sighed and rolled his eyes.

"Pray do not insist that I do something such as that without giving me an explanation. Before you begin, I should state that I do not have any particular interest in

Lady Helen and only sought her out because I believed her entirely unattached."

Lord Westerly's expression did not change.

"She *is* entirely unattached, but I fully intend to attach myself to her," he said, firmly. "Do you understand?"

A little irritated, Simon's jaw tightened.

"I do not enjoy being told what I must or must not do, Westerly. I do believe that a young lady ought to be able to decide for herself."

"You intend to push yourself forward, then?" Lord Westerly's brows fell low over his eyes. "Despite what I have asked you, despite what I have said, you will do whatever you wish without even thinking of what might befall others?"

"I have no interest in injuring anyone, but I shall not pull myself back from dancing with an eligible young lady and allowing *her* to decide whether or not she wishes to continue with our acquaintance." Still angered, Simon spoke with a sharpness that had not been in his voice before. "I am tired of gentlemen coming to tell me that I must not continue with this acquaintance, or I must step back from another. Leave me be, Westerly, and do not dare demand such things of me again."

With these words, he turned around and stalked away from Lord Westerly, growing frustrated with the gentleman's manner. This was now the second time he had been told to stay away from a lady, albeit without any particular reason as to why he ought to do so, save for the fact that another gentleman wished to be in her company which, to Simon's mind, was no reason at all. Letting out a heavy sigh, he shook his head, turned his gaze straight ahead, and realized that he was walking directly towards Lady Alice.

Her eyes caught his and, with a smile, she took a step forward... and Simon hesitated.

Should I go to speak with a wallflower?

His heart turned over in his chest as Lady Alice paused, her smile beginning to dim as she watched his face. No doubt she had thought he was coming to speak with her and after what he had done by way of defending her, he quite understood that.

Whether he was to go now or not, however, was quite a different question. His reputation had been bolstered by his defense of the lady but at the same time, the *ton* would not look upon him with as much of an interest should he linger long in the lady's company. This new interest in him presented him with further acquaintances, with those who would look upon him with intrigue, and it was *those* acquaintances he wanted to pursue, not the nearness of a wallflower. He was trying to make the very best match he could, and spending time with a wallflower would make that a little more difficult, would it not?

And yet, despite the thoughts in his mind, despite his desire to stay back and turn away, Simon's feet pushed him forward, closer to the young lady, and his heart began to sing as her smile slowly started to spread back across her face. He could not seem to pull himself away from her now, could not tug his heart back, and before he knew it, he was bowing, and she was curtseying.

"Lord Sedgewick, I am so very grateful for what you

did, saving me from Lord Cartwright's unwelcome interest."

Lady Alice bobbed another quick curtsey, then lifted her gaze to his, albeit with a good deal more tenderness in her expression than he had anticipated.

"There is no need to thank me again," he told her. "I was glad to be able to put Lord Cartwright away from you."

Her eyes closed tightly, and her smile wobbled a little.

"I do not think that you understand the significance of your actions. My reputation is already poor – although not by my own doing – and had anyone seen what Lord Cartwright was attempting to do, they might well have thought that I was eager and willing, which would have quite ruined me."

Simon's heart tore for her, seeing the pain in her eyes, and realizing now just how unfair the situation was. She had done nothing to become a wallflower, and yet society was treating her as though she bore the same guilt as her father.

"I am all the more glad to have been able to defend you, then." When she smiled, Simon found his lips quirking in response, pushing away the murmur of concern that grew within him as he spoke. "I was also sorry to hear of your father's circumstances and now, to see how they affect you, I am saddened to witness it." Clearing his throat as a nudge of guilt ripped through his heart, aware that he was just as bad as every other gentleman and lady in London, given how he considered the lady in question, Simon gestured to the dance floor.

"Might I ask you to dance, Lady Alice? I... oh." Squeezing his eyes closed, he bit his lip. "Forgive me, I quite forgot that I am entirely taken up this evening."

"That is quite all right." Lady Alice looked away. "Your consideration is a kindness enough."

"At the next ball, we shall dance," Simon said, before he even had time to think of what it was that he was saying. "I insist upon it."

His mind instantly began to scream at him, his thoughts spiraling in one direction and then the next, beginning to worry about what would be said of him when the *ton* recognized that he was standing up with a wallflower.

But the words had been said. And he could not turn away from her now.

"You are *most* generous." The warmth in Lady Alice's face, the sheer joy in her smile, had him returning her smile yet again, his concern still meandering its way through him but countered a little by the happiness he now felt at her acceptance. "Thank you, Lord Sedgewick. Yet again, you show me a great kindness."

"Not at all."

Harrumphing a little, to remove both the embarrassment and the guilt from him, he bowed quickly and turned to take his leave, aware of just how rapidly his heart was beating as he left Lady Alice's side.

"Was that the wallflower I saw you speaking with?" Lord Larbert leaned in towards Simon, emerging out of the shadows somewhere and making Simon jump in surprise. "You had gone to see that she was quite well, I suppose?"

"Precisely."

"And is she?"

"Is she what?"

"Well?" Lord Larbert chuckled. "Is she *well*?"

Flushing, Simon nodded and shot a dark look towards Lord Larbert.

"I do not know what it is that you are attempting to imply, but I can assure you, I have only concern for Lady Alice, nothing more."

"Is that so?"

Hating the lilt in his friend's voice, Simon nodded firmly.

"I am quite certain."

"Then why is it that she is the only one who, thus far, has made you smile so broadly that, even as you turn away from her, your eyes are alight and your expression joyous?"

Simon quickly attempted to rearrange his features, but it was much too late. Lord Larbert laughed aloud and Simon's face heated, but try as he might, he could not remove the smile from his face – even though it was, in part, a self-conscious one. He could not deny it from himself, just as he could not deny it from Lord Larbert.

Lady Alice had caught his interest and it seemed that now, there was nothing he could do about it.

CHAPTER SEVEN

I am to dance with Lord Sedgewick.
"You look a little starry-eyed this evening, which is most unusual for a wallflower." Lady Frederica smiled and slipped her arm through Alice's as they wandered around the ballroom together, with Miss Bosworth and Miss Fairley behind them. "I thought you might have quite the opposite expression, given that you were quite alone for the last few occasions."

Alice smiled and decided to tell her friend the truth.

"You heard about what happened with Lord Cartwright, of course," she began, having already told all of her fellow wallflowers about Lord Cartwright's treatment of her and how Lord Sedgewick had been the one to intervene. "I spoke with Lord Sedgewick some two days ago to thank him again for what he had done – and he told me that he wished to dance with me!"

Lady Frederica stopped at once, turning to face Alice with eyes wide open.

"To dance with you? Here? This evening?"

Alice nodded fervently.

"He asked to dance with me that very evening itself, only to recall that he was already engaged for every dance. Thus, he promised that we would dance at the next ball – and given that I have already spied him here this evening, it shall have to be tonight!"

The whirlwind of excitement that rose within her had her giggling as though she were nothing but a childish girl making her come out, overcome with the anticipation of all that an evening would hold, rather than a wallflower who had only one dance taken this evening.

"Oh, how wonderful!" Lady Frederica exclaimed, her hands grasping Alice's. "You must be very excited indeed!"

"I am." Alice giggled again and then tried to steady herself, aware that she could not lose herself in nervousness, not when Lord Sedgewick was to be seeking her out. "I think him an exceptionally kind gentleman... though a dance does not mean a great deal, I know."

Lady Frederica lifted one shoulder.

"It may mean more than you might permit yourself to believe," she said, with a small smile. "He has already come to your defense, as you have said. What if there is more to his interest than you expect?"

Alice shook her head, refusing to let herself begin to even think such thoughts, for fear of being gravely disappointed.

"No, I shall be grateful for whatever dance it is that I am to dance with him, and that shall be all. I am sure it is only another kindness, and nothing more."

Her friend did not immediately agree. Instead, she tipped her head and considered before speaking again.

"I think that we must permit ourselves a little hope if we are to have any enjoyment from the Season at all," she began, as though she had read Alice's thoughts as to why she could *not* permit herself to do so. "A gentleman has stated that he *will* dance with you, and will not permit himself to do anything other than that. To have such attention is an excellent thing! Besides which, Lord Sedgewick is a very *handsome* gentleman, and that cannot be denied."

Unable to help herself, Alice giggled again and tucked her arm into Lady Frederica's.

"I will agree with you on that."

"Look!" Lady Frederica stopped again, pulling Alice to a halt. "Is that not him? Is he not, at this very moment, coming to speak with you?"

Alice's mouth went dry, and she could not form a response. Instead, she could only stare as Lord Sedgewick came closer and closer, though his gaze was not resting on her face. Rather, he looked from side to side, seemingly unaware that she was there – unless it was that he was simply doing so to be polite to those who came near him.

"Lord Sedgewick, good evening!" Lady Frederica trilled, though Alice quickly tugged at her arm, begging her in low tones to be quiet, but Lady Frederica, seeming now to be filled with courage, called out again, greeting him warmly. Alice's face burned hot, and she looked away, uncertain as to what it was that she could say, other than to beg an apology from him for her friend's forwardness.

"Lady... Frederica, is it not?" Lord Sedgewick frowned, then bowed when she nodded. "And Lady Alice. Good evening." Clearing his throat, he put his hands behind his back. "Pray, forgive me. I was only–"

"I hear that you are to dance with Lady Alice this evening."

Alice closed her eyes and took a quick breath, her heart fluttering as she wondered what it was her friend was thinking, in speaking to him in such a way. This was not at all necessary, for Lord Sedgewick was already aware that they were to dance and, to her mind, did not need to be reminded of it.

And then she opened her eyes and doubt flooded her. Lord Sedgewick was frowning, his mouth tugged to one side and lines puckering his forehead.

He has forgotten.

Her heart sank, dropping to shatter on the floor as she looked away from him, her face now burning with mortification. She said not a word, leaving silence to fill the space between them.

"Ah, yes! The dance!" Now it was Lord Sedgewick's turn to look embarrassed, waving one hand frantically as if he had always remembered that there was to be a dance, but had only now brought it into conversation. "Yes, we were to dance this evening, Lady Alice, were we not? Of course. Yes, I recall. Now, I think that the..." Looking around him, he coughed lightly and then looked back at her, though Alice could barely bring her eyes to his. "What should you say to the polka?"

"The polka, my Lord?" Alice swallowed, trying to recall if she knew how to dance the polka. Of course, she had stepped into the dance last Season but that had been so very long ago, and she had spent this Season doing nothing other than watching others dance it. "Yes, of course. I–"

"No, that will not do."

Alice blinked as Lord Sedgewick pulled out his dance card, where the gentlemen would keep a record of the young ladies they were to step out with, and ran one finger over his mouth as he frowned down at it.

"Ah, as I thought, I am to step out with Lady Gillian for the polka. Which means that I... oh."

Her heart sinking, Alice closed her eyes and took a breath before feigning a cheerful expression and sending a smile into her voice – a smile that she did not feel in any way whatsoever.

"Lord Sedgewick, pray do not concern yourself. If you are unable to step out with me, then I quite understand. There is no need to do so, not when, as I am sure, you have many other eligible young ladies seeking you out. Please, there is no concern nor sadness on my part, to be sure."

A look of relief passed over Lord Sedgewick's expression, the tension leaving his shoulders, but before he could say anything, Lady Frederica leaned over and, in much too bold a manner, let out an exclamation and jabbed one finger at his dance card.

"Ah, but Lord Sedgewick has the waltz remaining, my dear friend! So you are to have your dance after all." A broad grin on her face, she winked at Alice though, much to Alice's relief, Lord Sedgewick did not see it. "Ah! And it is only a short time away, for they have just stepped out for the country dance and the waltz is to come thereafter."

Alice did not know what to say, or what to do. Lord Sedgewick's mouth opened and then closed again, his eyes turning from her to Lady Frederica before going back to his dance card as though, miraculously, something would have changed in the few short moments between Lady Frederica speaking of it, and his eyes going to see it.

There was no escape for him, however, and though Alice knew she ought to be glad that she was to dance with the gentleman after all, all she felt was embarrassment. It was clear to her, at least, that Lord Sedgewick had no real interest in dancing with her, and had been glad to be freed from his obligation to her, whereas now, he had no choice but to offer the one and only dance he had remaining – the waltz – which, she was sure, he had kept free so that he might choose carefully the lady he was to step out with. Certainly, he would not want to dance the waltz with a wallflower!

"Yes, it seems that the waltz does remain." Lord Sedgewick let out a huff of breath and looked at her, his eyes searching hers, though no smile came to his face. "Then we are to dance the waltz, Lady Alice. Will you be content with that?"

"Yes, of course."

There was no other response she could give, and though Lord Sedgewick nodded, Alice's heart twisted with the sharp pain that came with his obvious disappointment. Yes, he was doing his utmost to hide it from her, but it could not be easily pushed aside. Who was it that he had hoped to dance with, she wondered silently. Was it a specific young lady? Was it someone he thought of often? A young lady who was quickly becoming the apple of his eye?

Perhaps I ought to refuse him.

As though she knew exactly what it was that Alice was thinking, Lady Frederica smiled and put a hand on her arm.

"I will be very glad to see you stepping out with such a fine gentleman, Lady Alice," she said, loud enough for Lord Sedgewick to hear. "After all, it is just as you deserve. Society ought not to be punishing you for your father's misdeeds, as I am sure Lord Sedgewick will agree."

"My Lord?"

Before Alice or Lord Sedgewick could say anything, a footman arrived with a tray upon which was placed only a single glass. Alice looked away, a flush rising up her chest and into her face as she realized that the footman was ignoring both herself and Lady Frederica, as though they were completely invisible, hidden from his eyes simply because they were wallflowers.

"I thank you."

Lord Sedgewick took the glass from the tray and Alice watched him as he took a sip of the brandy, wishing that she had found a way to refuse the waltz in a manner which would not have been viewed as improper or impolite.

"Do try and smile." Lady Frederica squeezed her hand as Alice continued to watch Lord Sedgewick, seeing how quickly he tipped the brandy down his throat.

"You are to waltz! I know it is some time since you have done so but it is simple enough. Just permit Lord Sedgewick to lead you."

Alice looked at her friend.

"He does not wish to waltz with me, I am sure of it." Keeping her voice low, she closed her eyes tightly as Lady Frederica shrugged. "It was to be for some other young lady, I think."

"And now it is yours." There was a firmness in Lady Frederica's voice which Alice did not feel, though she appreciated her friend's determination. It bolstered her courage a little and she lifted her chin. "You are doing nothing wrong. Instead, you are taking what was promised you, and there can be no shame in that. It would have been wrong for Lord Sedgewick to stand away from you, or to refuse to stand up with you even though he had a dance remaining. Come now, do try and smile! Enjoy this moment. It may not come again."

Before Alice had a moment to reply, the waltz was called and, as she lifted her eyes to Lord Sedgewick, she saw how he set the glass back on a nearby footman's tray before, with a grimace, coming close to her again.

"There was a strange foulness in that brandy," he muttered, offering her his hand. "Well then, Lady Alice. Shall we step out together?"

She nodded, her stomach twisting this way and that, and even though Lady Frederica smiled at her, even though there was a happiness in her own heart trying to push through her worry and concern, she could not bring such a smile to her lips. Shrinking inwardly, aware that a good many of the guests would be taking note of her *and*

Lord Sedgewick as they stood up together, she did her best to keep her gaze fixed straight ahead and her expression set.

"Thank you for this dance, Lord Sedgewick," she murmured, as she dropped into a curtsey and he into his bow. "I do appreciate your kindness."

For the first time since they had begun their discussion, Lord Sedgewick smiled and, in doing so, softened his entire expression. In that one moment, her worries began to tear apart and fade away and when she stepped into his arms, the tension in her frame grew less and less until he was the only person in the entire ballroom. She could barely hear the music, such was the sheer joy of being in a gentleman's arms again, and when he began to step, she flowed with him easily, her feet in time with his and her hand clasping his tightly.

Lord Sedgewick's blue eyes reminded her of the sky on a cloudless day, with flickers of light coming into them as though the sun was reflected in them. His fair hair shifted lightly, brushing across his forehead as they danced and suddenly, Alice's breath caught and snared in her chest, her heart beginning to pound with an entirely new sensation. She could not seem to pull her gaze away from his, could not seem to take even the quickest look away from him and, as the dance continued, the sensations within her only grew. Surely this was only because of the dance, she told herself, only because she was dancing the waltz with a gentleman for the first time in so many months! And yet, when Lord Sedgewick smiled, it was as if her heart tore itself out of her chest, flung itself up to the skies, and refused to come down again.

From the first moment that she had seen him, Alice had thought Lord Sedgewick the most handsome gentleman she had ever seen but now, standing close to him, his arm at her waist, she could not even put her thoughts into coherent order. His gaze swept over her face, and it was as if he knew everything she was thinking, that small smile tugging at his mouth an indication that he was enjoying their dance almost as much as she.

And then, he stumbled.

All that she felt, all that had risen within her, flung itself back down again and Alice took in a deep breath, wondering at Lord Sedgewick's sudden frown.

"Forgive me, Lady Alice." Lord Sedgewick cleared his throat and turned his head away, looking out across the ballroom as they danced. "It is only that I... oh, good gracious!"

Alice's face grew hot as Lord Sedgewick danced to the corner of the room before bringing their waltz to a stop while everyone else continued on. Angry at her own foolishness, she looked away from him, sure now that he had decided to end their waltz because they were garnering far too much attention.

"I do apologize, Lord Sedgewick. I ought not to have insisted on the waltz."

A tight hand grasped her arm and Alice's head spun around to look at Lord Sedgewick again, only for alarm to flare at the sight of him.

"It is not that, Lady Alice," he groaned, one arm clamped around his waist. "It is not that I wished to end our waltz for my own sake. It is because I did not wish to embarrass you by collapsing into a puddle on the floor... much as I fear I shall do now!"

"You require a physician!" Exclaiming aloud, Alice looked around, catching the eye of a gentleman who looked on only to see him hurrying towards them. "Whatever is wrong, Lord Sedgewick?"

He groaned again and then, spying a chair, staggered towards it before sitting down heavily.

"I do not know."

Leaning forward, he let out a sharp exclamation, just as the other gentleman reached them both – a gentleman that Alice recognized as Lord Larbert.

"Whatever is the matter, old boy?" he asked, bending forward so he might speak to Lord Sedgewick in his doubled-over state. "Do you need fortifying?"

"He does not need more liquor!" Alice exclaimed, a hand on Lord Larbert's, pulling him back. "A physician! You must fetch the physician at once. Lord Sedgewick is ill and is clearly weak and in pain. Might you be able to send for one?"

Lord Larbert looked back at her for a moment or two but, much to Alice's relief, did not argue.

"But of course. I will go to speak to our host and have Lord Sedgewick taken to a smaller room." He smiled tightly. "And might I suggest, Lady Alice, that you go back to your friends? I speak not for his sake but for your own."

Heat billowed in her face, and she looked away, back to Lord Sedgewick, understanding precisely what it was Lord Larbert meant. He was warning her to be careful of what could be seen and what, thereafter, could be said about her. After all, if Lord Sedgewick had become ill while dancing with her, then would not society think to blame her for it? They could whisper that being in company with a wallflower had been the reason for his sudden illness and laugh that Lord Sedgewick would never dare do the same thing again! A vision of what her future might be like should she linger reared up and she turned away quickly, only to hesitate and look back at Lord Sedgewick. She could not leave him when Lord Larbert had stepped away also, could she?

"I – I will send a note tomorrow, if I may, to see how you fare," she murmured, coming closer to him again and refusing to be pushed away by the fears which lingered in her heart, set there by Lord Larbert's warning. "I am sorry to step away, but I fear that I must."

Lord Sedgewick's blue eyes were shadowed now, dark and stormy.

"Please." Much to her surprise, his hand lifted and found hers, though quite how he had managed to do so when he was clearly in a good deal of discomfort, Alice was not quite certain. "Do not concern yourself on my account. I am certain all will be well."

She did not know what to do, the sudden, swift action of his hand on hers making the urge to leave drift away. The connection, the intensity she had felt before during their dance began to rekindle itself, even though Alice herself knew it was an entirely inappropriate moment for it to do so.

"Here is our host." Lord Larbert returned to Lord Sedgewick's side and Alice quickly dropped Lord Sedgewick's hand, catching the glance Lord Larbert sent in her direction and, thereafter, making to step away. "Come now, Sedgewick, we will send for the physician and all will be quite well."

Alice melted back into the shadows quickly enough, certain that no one would look at her now that she was back where wallflowers were meant to be. Her hands clasped together, her fingers at her mouth as she watched Lord Larbert help Lord Sedgewick from the chair and walked back through the ballroom to the door. Her worry returned, her heart pounding with concern.

Just what had happened to Lord Sedgewick?

CHAPTER EIGHT

"Whatever it was, it is over now."
Simon resisted the desire to roll his eyes in the physician's direction.

"Yes, I am well aware of that."

"It seems very strange." The physician drummed on the edge of the table with his fingers, and Simon found himself irritated by the sound, though he did not say anything. "You must have imbibed or ingested something which caused the discomfort."

Lord Larbert, who had returned at the very earliest hour he could manage - which, conveniently, happened to be at the same time as the physician had returned to make certain that Simon was quite well, frowned heavily.

"You mean to say that there was something in whatever Lord Sedgewick ate last evening? Or drank?"

The physician nodded.

"That would be my suspicion, yes."

"But then surely a great many other people would be unwell." Getting up out of his chair, Lord Larbert gestured first to Simon and then back to the physician. "Given how Lord Sedgewick is this morning – well but still weak and tired – I would have expected to hear reports of other gentlemen and ladies suffering in the same manner. In fact, I should have expected myself to be as unwell also, mayhap!"

Simon nodded quickly.

"Yes, I quite agree. Given that the food and drink served at the ball would have been offered to every guest, then, as Lord Larbert says, you would have been called to another few houses at least!"

"And I have not been called to any," the physician admitted, rising to his feet. "However, I am glad that you are recovered, my Lord. I will take my leave of you. Should you have need, please do send for me again."

Choosing not to get out of his chair, Simon held out one hand and the physician shook it firmly.

"Thank you. Please make sure to send your account at once, and I will have it paid by the day's end."

He did not miss the glint that came into the physician's eyes as he promised he would do so, knowing full well that the man would charge him a substantial fee for his services, though Simon had to admit that he had helped him to recover. He had been taken home last evening, and the physician had given him a dark, disgusting concoction to drink then, once he had finished the last drop, Simon had promptly cast up his accounts - though the physician had appeared rather pleased with that result. Since then, though he had been fatigued and a little cold, the pain that had bitten hard in his stomach and the agony that had spread long, hard fingers through his body had begun to dissipate until he had been able to sleep. This morning, there was not a single trace of the pain, and Simon had been very grateful indeed for that.

"So, what are we to make of all of this?" Lord Larbert walked back across the parlor and sat down heavily, his frown still pulling down his features. "There is something untoward about all of this, which I do not like."

"You were not the one suffering," Simon returned, though this was said with a wry smile. "In truth, Larbert, I do not know *what* to make of it. All was well, I danced with Lady Alice, and in the middle of the waltz, I was overcome by such pain that I was forced to stop. Thank heavens I did not collapse in the middle of the dance floor and bring Lady Alice down with me! She has suffered enough indignity already!"

"It was very strange," Lord Larbert murmured, his eyes darting around the room, clearly deep in thought about what had happened and what might now be the reason for it. "You do not think... no, I am sure it could not be."

Simon frowned.

"If you are thinking of placing the burden of blame upon Lady Alice, then I should like you to remove that thought from your mind at once. She is certainly *not* responsible. After all, how could she be?"

Lord Larbert shrugged.

"How could anyone be responsible for it?"

With a scowl, Simon looked away, wishing that he could find an answer to that particular question. "Something I imbibed or ingested, the physician said."

"Which could be any number of things," his friend

added, quickly. "I am sure that you ate and drank a great deal."

With a sigh, Simon nodded.

"I did."

"Then what is there to say? Perhaps it was purely an unfortunate circumstance – *you* were the unlucky one who ate something which was not meant to be eaten, and then quickly become ill because of it."

"You mean to suggest that, out of every guest at that one ball, *I* was the one who picked up and ate something in particular which made me ill." When his friend nodded, Simon let out another sigh and then nodded. "Very well, let us say that I agree with you on that. I cannot see or think of any other reason as to why I might have become so unwell."

"Save for someone ensuring that you ate or drank something noxious, deliberately – which, I think, would be not only difficult to do, but which also I can see no reason for – I think that is the best answer we shall have to your sudden illness and the most reasonable explanation. Though I am glad to see that it is gone from you now, at least."

"That is a relief, yes."

A tap came at the door, and Simon called for the servant to enter, only for the butler to hurry in and murmur something in his ear which made Simon's eyebrows lift so very high that Lord Larbert's attention was caught in an instant.

"What is it?" he demanded, as Simon began to smile. "Why did you look so surprised?"

"If she will come in, then pray do ask her to step in

for a few minutes. Tell her that Lord Larbert is present also, so she will not be concerned." Speaking to the butler, Simon turned his attention back to his friend. "It seems that Lady Alice has come to call on me."

Lord Larbert's eyebrows rose.

"Lady Alice? Has come here alone?"

"Yes, with just a maid, but you are not to make any remarks which might make her uncomfortable," Simon stated, firmly. "She sought only to ask one of my staff how I fared this morning, but the butler came to tell me of her presence, and I am glad that he did. I wish very much to reassure her that all is well."

The recollection of how he had reached out to take her hand, how he had held onto it so tightly and felt her gentle warmth. Despite the pain he still felt, he found himself smiling, only to catch Lord Larbert's grin. With a sniff, he pushed himself out of the chair and turned to the door, ready to greet the lady... and aware of the swell of anticipation that grew within him as every second passed.

The door opened and the butler announced her name, but it took Lady Alice a few seconds to appear. She came cautiously, walking slowly into the room, her brown eyes wide with clear concern and her lip caught between her teeth. Her maid slipped in behind her, and stood quietly by the door, serving propriety's purposes without intruding on their conversation.

"I am quite well, I assure you." Smiling, Simon came closer to her, spreading his arms out wide in welcome. "Please, do come in. Would you like me to send for a tea tray? I would be glad to have your company for a little while."

Lady Alice's face flooded with relief; she looked him in the eye and smiled.

"Oh, Lord Sedgewick, I am very glad to see you so recovered. To be truthful, I was a little concerned as to what state I might find you in this morning, but I am delighted to see you feeling better."

"Thank you for your aid last evening." Aware that he was still standing – and that he was growing fatigued rather quickly, Simon gestured to a chair and then smiled. "Please, do sit down, even if only for a few minutes." Seeing her hesitation, he smiled again. "Mayhap you will be able to offer your thoughts as regards what took place last evening. Lord Larbert and I have come to some conclusions, but we still struggle to understand precisely what made me so unwell." This seemed to be enough to convince Lady Alice and, after greeting Lord Larbert, she moved to sit down, though her hands clasped tight in her lap and her eyes darted from Lord Larbert to Simon and then back again, clearly a little uncertain that she was doing as she ought. Simon kept his smile on his face, hoping that it would encourage the lady to be at ease. "Thank you, Lady Alice. Now, if you wish, I shall tell you what the physician said and, thereafter, what Lord Larbert and I have been discussing." When she nodded, he quickly laid out an explanation of all that had been said and watched as her eyes fastened themselves on his and her frame softened just a little as she listened. "Thus, you now find us wondering whether or not it was a mere mishap, a circumstance which might have happened to anyone but, unfortunately, happened to me – or something else."

Lady Alice did not immediately respond. Instead, she looked from Simon to Lord Larbert and then spread her hands.

"It would be the most reasonable and understandable explanation, I think."

"Which is what I said already," Lord Larbert stated, a hint of triumph in his voice.

"Yes, I am aware that you did." Simon rolled his eyes but grinned. "You see, Lady Alice, it seems as though we are in a place where the only answer *must* be that it was an accident."

"There is also the possibility that it was a deliberate act, however," she added before he could say anything more. "I suppose, if you were to consider that, you should then begin to ask yourself who would do such a thing and why."

The gentle lift of her eyebrow had him suddenly going very hot indeed, sitting forward in his chair and responding with such fierceness that even Lord Larbert looked surprised.

"I do not have any enemies, Lady Alice," Simon found himself saying, words pouring out of him now. "I have never done anything to garner any sort of malicious response. I am not a gentleman with dark secrets, nor someone who behaves with any sort of ill intent towards anyone, I can assure you of that. If someone *has* done this deliberately, then mayhap they did so with the hope of giving it to someone else – and *I* was the unfortunate one who took it by accident."

The silence that came once his speech was ended had the heat in Simon's face growing all the hotter, to the point that he had to drop his gaze and look away, finding the floor to be of greater interest than looking either in Lady Alice or Lord Larbert's direction.

"I quite agree with Lord Sedgewick." Lord Larbert harrumphed, then chuckled, making Simon wince with mortification. "It is just as he has said. He is not at all the sort of fellow who would gain any real enemies, given that he is always amiable and considerate." When Simon slid his gaze to his friend, Lord Larbert only laughed again. "Come now, my friend, does that calm your worry? I have defended you to Lady Alice, though I do not think that she thinks poorly of you if that is your concern."

In an instant, Lady Alice's eyes flew wide, and she caught her breath, turning her gaze to meet Simon's, who found himself quite unable to look away.

"Oh, goodness, I did not mean to imply that there was any sort of darkness about you, Lord Sedgewick. When I said that someone might have done such a thing to you deliberately, it was not because I thought you a disreputable sort who did nothing other than cause pain and strife to others! I do not believe you are the sort of gentleman who would ever find himself with a great number of enemies."

Even though he was mortified at having made such an emphatic reply, which was now followed by Lady Alice's fevered response, Simon caught himself smiling back at her, seemingly glad that she thought so well of him. Why her opinion of him should matter, Simon did not know but, all the same, he was glad of it.

"I appreciate that consideration, Lady Alice."

"I should think that, if it was a deliberate act, it was

done with the intention of it being given to someone else," Lady Alice finished, getting to her feet as a wave of disappointment broke across Simon, now that she was to take her leave. "I am very glad to see you recovered, Lord Sedgewick. I should return to my carriage now."

"We will dance again, however." Lady Alice turned just as Simon attempted to understand what it was that he had been trying to say. The words had left his mouth before he had even had time to think about what it was that he really wanted to say. Swirling brown eyes looked back into his and Simon's stomach lurched, as he felt himself pulled towards her, though he stayed precisely where he was, albeit with a good deal of effort. "I should like to dance with you again if you would like to." Ignoring Lord Larbert entirely, he turned to face Lady Alice a little more. "Our first dance was rudely interrupted, and I think that it would only be right to make certain that we stand up together again."

Lady Alice said nothing for some moments, but Simon did not miss the way a gentle sheen came into her eyes. His heart softened for her again, finding himself inwardly wondering why it was thought fair of society to push such a delightful creature away, simply because her father had behaved poorly.

"You are a very kind gentleman, Lord Sedgewick." When Lady Alice finally spoke, her voice was quiet with clear waves of emotion running through it. "If you truly wish to dance with me again, then I will, of course, accept, but I do not want you to do so out of obligation. I assure you, I will be perfectly contented with the dance – or most of the dance – that we shared together."

Simon shook his head.

"No, I will not be contented with that, Lady Alice. At the next ball, I shall have your name down for the waltz, and this time, I hope, we shall dance all of it without interruption."

The smile that spread across her face almost dazzled him. Her eyes were alight with happiness, her hands clasping together at her heart. The joy he had brought her by such a small, simple action was almost too much for Simon to accept, for surely, to his mind, she deserved such a thing as this. She deserved to be noticed, to be accepted by society, deserved to be treated as any other young lady might.

Do I think such a way because I truly believe it or because my heart is, for whatever reason, delighted in her company?

"Thank you, Lord Sedgewick. I look forward to dancing with you again."

"As do I."

The smile that lingered long on his lips and the way his eyes fixed themselves on her as she walked from the room, followed by her maid, told Simon that there was more to his connection to the lady than he wanted to admit. With a small frown flickering across his forehead, he sat down again and did his best to ignore Lord Larbert's broad smile.

"Lady Alice is a lovely young lady, I must say."

Simon shot a look toward Lord Larbert.

"You are seeking to ask me something in making such a statement as that."

"And if I am?"

"Then I will not rise to it," Simon returned, quickly. "I am only doing what is right for me to do as a gentleman. It was not her fault that our dance came to an end so quickly and, given that she is a wallflower, it seems unfair to her to leave it at that. I must do what is right, must I not?"

"I suppose you must." The grin had not faded, but Simon looked away, then rose to ring the bell. "I think I must eat something."

Lord Larbert's smile faded.

"Then do you feel a little better?"

"A good deal better, in fact."

"The wonders of a visit from a very pretty young lady," Lord Larbert murmured, as Simon tugged at the bell pull. "Perhaps you ought to ask Lady Alice to come to call again so that you might regain your strength all the faster!"

"Mayhap I shall," Simon responded quickly, seeing Lord Larbert's look of surprise. "Come now, no more jesting. I want to be entirely back to health by tomorrow evening so that I might attend Lord Hearthstone's ball."

"Where you hope Lady Alice will be present also, no doubt."

Simon ignored this and sat back down with a small sigh, though his heart jumped about inside his chest, telling him that what his friend had said was precisely what he was hoping for.

CHAPTER NINE

"You say he took unwell?"

"Yes, but he has recovered. He said…" Dampening down her excitement, Alice leaned in closer to her friend. "He told me that he would dance with me again and that this time, the waltz would not be interrupted!"

Lady Frederica's eyes widened.

"Is that so?"

"Yes, and he made certain to promise it in front of Lord Larbert so he cannot change his mind now!"

"How altered he is from the first time you were to dance with him," Lady Frederica murmured, as they stood together at the side of the ballroom. "I knew I was being very bold indeed in speaking as I did, but I could not help it! I wanted you to dance with the gentleman and he appeared to have forgotten – which I could not abide! Therefore, I spoke with as much boldness as I dared and now look what has come of it! You are to have another dance!"

Alice giggled and then pressed her hand to her mouth as though to push back the sound.

"I should not permit myself to be so foolish, I know, but I am rather excited. The first time, I was full of nothing but worry about stepping out with him, but the moment the music began, it was as though everyone else was gone from me and only I and Lord Sedgewick were standing there together. It was a very strange sensation – which was then entirely removed from me once I realized how unwell he had become!"

Lady Frederica's smile broke, pressing down into a thin line.

"That is very strange indeed. Did he say if there was any reason given for it?"

Shaking her head, Alice offered her friend a wry smile.

"The physician says that it was something which he either ate or drank which made him so very unwell, though quite what that could be, he does not know. It may have been a mistake from the kitchens, though it might also have been deliberate – though why someone would wish to injure him in such a way, I cannot imagine."

"No, nor can I."

With a few seconds of silence passing between them, Alice glanced at her friend and then away again.

"He did seem pleased to see me."

"Of course he did!" Lady Frederica's exclamation seemed to echo across the ballroom and Alice shushed her quickly, though her friend only smiled. "And it is quite natural for you to have... a gentle affection for him, if that is what is within your heart."

Not in the least bit embarrassed or upset that Lady Frederica seemed to understand what she was feeling, Alice let out a small breath and nodded.

"I do feel something, I will admit, though quite what it is, I am not certain. It could easily be gratitude and nothing more."

"Though I doubt that it is," Lady Frederica responded, quickly. "You have taken notice of him since you first saw him and *that* speaks of an interest that is a good deal more profound than mere gratitude. My dear friend, it is as though a spark has caught you and you are now alight! There is a brightness to your smile and a happiness in your eyes that was not there before now. Is Lord Sedgewick to blame for it all?"

"Yes, though I do not know if it is fair to blame him for it." With a small smile, Alice let her gaze drift away across the ballroom. "I confess to being a little uncertain about my feelings at present. It is foolishness to permit myself any of the sort, given that I am a wallflower and he a Marquess."

"A Marquess who has chosen to speak with you on many occasions and is now to dance with you," came the response as Alice flushed just a little. "He might easily have stated that the dance you shared, albeit incomplete, was enough, but he has not. Instead, he insists on dancing with you again, to make certain that you dance an entire waltz together! That will be noted by some in the *ton*, I can assure you, but that does not seem to dissuade him."

"It does not dissuade me at all."

With a yelp of surprise, Alice turned sharply, only to practically fall into the arms of Lord Sedgewick who had spoken just behind her. With a chuckle, he put one hand out to steady her, the other holding a glass of brandy.

"Good evening, Lady Alice. I came to see if your waltz was still available for me to take? As I have promised, I would like to stand up with you again."

"You are very kind, Lord Sedgewick." A little embarrassed at her reaction and with the touch of his hand on her arm bringing her a flush of heat that ran all the way up to her heart, Alice dropped her head and looked away. "I do hope that you have recovered entirely?"

"I have, I thank you." Lord Sedgewick cleared his throat and then bowed. "And good evening to you also, Lady Frederica. How do you fare?"

Lady Frederica let out a slightly harsh laugh.

"Given that I am a wallflower who is attempting to be a little bolder by merely walking around a ballroom rather than hiding away, I am not as happy as I might be, Lord Sedgewick. Though I am a little happier than I was at the beginning of the Season."

"That is something, at least."

"And I am glad that you have offered to dance again with Lady Alice," Lady Frederica finished, offering a quick wink to Alice, making it quite clear that she was going to be just as bold as she had been before. "I think that quite wonderful."

"Thank you, Lady Frederica." Lord Sedgewick grinned, his face lit with his smile and Alice's heart thundered furiously, forcing her to look away for fear that he would notice her reaction. Their previous nearness demanded more from her now, bringing her attention back towards him with a strength that hadn't been there before now.

"The waltz, then?"

Lord Sedgewick's tone had softened, and Alice forced herself to look back at him, heat beginning to rise from her core, spreading out across her chest and up to her neck.

"That would be quite lovely, thank you." A nervous giggle threatened, and she managed to smile. "Let us hope that you are not unwell again, Lord Sedgewick, else I shall begin to think that you are doing it deliberately!"

"I would never do such a thing," he promised, putting one hand to his heart, a seriousness coming into his eyes again. "I look forward to our dance, Lady Alice. I mean every word of that, I assure you."

Alice's smile remained as Lord Sedgewick bowed and then turned away, though the moment he was gone from her presence, she grasped Lady Frederica's arm and bent her head low.

"Whatever am I to do? I cannot find myself drawn to Lord Sedgewick!"

"Yes, you can." Lady Frederica smiled and shrugged both shoulders lightly. "I am afraid, my dear, that we cannot help our hearts. Regardless of what it is that we feel we ought to do, or what even is wise, our hearts will lead us in directions we do not wish to go. I cannot tell you whether or not there is any happiness to be found in Lord Sedgewick's prolonged company but–"

"Of course there can be no happiness," Alice interrupted, suddenly angry with herself for what she felt and how ridiculous it was. "I am a wallflower, and he is a gentleman."

"And such things have happened before, I am sure. Look at Miss Bosworth! Is she not in company with a gentleman also?"

Alice hesitated before she responded. Lady Frederica was quite right, Miss Bosworth *was* in company with a gentleman very often, and thus far, while society had made a few remarks, their connection had continued – and was growing.

Can I hope for the same for myself?

"If you think well of Lord Sedgewick, then permit yourself to feel whatever is within your heart," Lady Frederica said quietly. "It is not wrong, nor is it foolishness. You cannot say what will come of it, I understand that, but trying to hide it away will do nothing other than torment you, I am sure."

Taking a deep breath, Alice nodded slowly and then managed to put on a slightly wry smile.

"I think that you are quite right, loath though I am to admit it. I would prefer it if I felt nothing at all. I feel as though all of society is peering at me, wondering what it is that I am doing, standing in front of them all and waltzing with a Marquess."

Lady Frederica smiled.

"They are, I am sure," she replied, making Alice's eyes widen. "But is that not what we are trying to do? We are attempting to push our way out of the shadows and instead, find our way back into society's view - whether they like our presence or not!"

With a slow nod, Alice took in a long, steadying breath and closed her eyes.

"You are quite right," she agreed, eventually. "I will do my utmost not to feel any nervousness when I dance with Lord Sedgewick again." Swallowing hard, she closed her eyes. "And I will let my heart free to feel whatever it desires when it comes to the Marquess himself."

∽

"I did enjoy our first waltz together."

Alice settled her hand in Lord Sedgewick's, all too aware of the sensations that built in her when he put his other hand to her waist.

"Thank you, Lord Sedgewick. I enjoyed it also."

"Then I am certain that this one will be all the more enjoyable, given that we shall dance all of it without interruption."

Moving quickly, Lord Sedgewick stepped into the first movement and soon, they were both spinning around the floor with ease.

Alice's heart sang.

"You dance very well, Lady Alice," he murmured, his hand tightening on hers just a little. "I think you... oh."

Her eyes flared, concern leaping up within her.

"Lord Sedgewick?"

"It is nothing. Just a twinge." With a smile, he continued with the dance though Alice did not miss the flickering shadows that leapt into his eyes. "It must have been some time since you stepped out to waltz with a gentleman, though

I mean no insult by saying such a thing." Offering him a small smile, Alice said nothing by way of response. "I would not have noticed anything, had I not been aware of your present circumstances." Perhaps aware that his remarks might have sounded a little insulting, Lord Sedgewick continued speaking, his words coming a little more quickly now. "As I have said, your dancing is wonderful."

"Thank you. You speak very kindly."

Slowly sinking into the happiness that seemed to surround her – and pushing aside the awareness of society's eyes upon them both, Alice let herself relax a little more, enjoying every moment of being in his arms. This was a wonderful situation and not one which was likely to repeat itself and thus, Alice decided she would relish every second of being in his arms. After this dance, would Lord Sedgewick seek her out again so that they might dance together? She did not think that he would.

"I – I am sorry, Lady Alice."

Her thoughts were pulled away from herself and she returned her attention to Lord Sedgewick, only to gasp at the whiteness of his face.

"Lord Sedgewick, are you–"

"I do not understand what has happened." Still dancing, the gentleman shook his head. "I am terribly sorry, Lady Alice, I fear I must... I must step away."

This time, he did not dance with her near a shadowy corner as he had done before but instead, simply dropped his hands from her and turned to make his way through the other dancers and back to the side of the ballroom. Alice stared after him, only to realize that she was now in a sea of dancers, adrift amongst them as she fought the panic that began to bite at her.

I cannot believe that this has happened again!

Curling her hands into tight fists, Alice began to make her way back in between the dancers, though she had to dodge and step away quickly so as not to knock into any of them. Her heart was pounding, her face hot and though she kept her head lowered and her gaze as close to the floor as she could, she did not doubt that everyone else who watched the dance would have noticed her hurrying away – and, no doubt, watched Lord Sedgewick doing the very same a few moments before her.

Whatever had happened? She had not expected there to be a second bout of illness, nor had she anticipated that Lord Sedgewick would hurry away from her and leave her standing in the middle of the ballroom without a partner. If she had been embarrassed to begin with, she was mortified now.

He did not do such a thing purposefully, she reminded herself, trying to make herself as small as possible as she squeezed and darted her way to the very edge of the ballroom. *He was ill...again.*

Closing her eyes in relief at the shadows that opened their arms to her, Alice leaned her head back against the wall and let out a long, slow breath. He had been perfectly well beforehand, and she had seen him stepping out with one or two other young ladies... so why, then, had he taken so ill when dancing with her?

"There you are. Whatever happened?" It was not only Lady Frederica who joined them but also Miss Fairley, her eyes rounding as she took Alice's hand and pressed it tight. "I saw you dancing with Lord Sedgewick, I looked away and then the next moment, he was gone, and you were scurrying back here!"

"Do you think everyone saw me?" Embarrassment coiled in her chest, and she looked away, struggling even to look at her friends. "I am so ashamed. Lord Sedgewick took ill and–"

"Again?" Lady Frederica's expression matched the shock in her voice. "Good gracious, whatever happened?"

"I do not know."

"You have no need to be ashamed, however," Lady Frederica continued, grasping Alice's other hand. "There is nothing that *you* have done to cause this."

"Precisely." Speaking with as much warmth in her voice as possible, Miss Fairley smiled encouragingly. "You did not do anything to make Lord Sedgewick ill, did you?"

Alice shook her head.

"Of course I did not."

"Then what troubles you?"

"The fact that he has danced *twice* with me and, after becoming ill on the first occasion, has now, on the second occasion, almost collapsed in the middle of the ballroom due to his ill health! It came on so suddenly and with such force, there was nothing for him to do but abandon me and our dance and thereafter, hurry away from the other dancers to the point that I do not know what has happened to him." Closing her eyes, she let out a low groan. "This is truly dreadful. Every gentleman and lady will, no doubt, be speaking of me and what has occurred

– and then I shall be the talk of London and will have to return home just as soon as is possible. My father's name will be all the more disgraced and–"

"Hush, now." Miss Fairley spoke with a firmness that cut through the rising panic in Alice's chest. "No such thing will occur, I assure you. While some will have noticed what has taken place, I am convinced that very few members of the *ton* will take any interest in it whatsoever."

There came a small smile on her face and, as Alice looked back at her, the smile began to spread, sending a twinkle into Miss Fairley's eye.

"Why do you say such a thing?" Alice asked slowly, as Miss Fairley grinned. "Something else has occurred, has it not?"

"Indeed. Miss Bosworth and a particular gentleman have been noticed by the *ton* and it is *they* who are being spoken of at present, not you." Lady Frederica immediately began to nod fervently, as though she had only just remembered that this had occurred. Relief climbed into Alice's panicked heart and slowly began to calm it, making her sag back against the wall again. "You will not even be noticed," Miss Fairley finished, making Alice smile a little wanly. "Come then, shall we see what has happened to Lord Sedgewick?"

Alice took another breath, a slight worry beginning to push into her veins and making her heart quicken.

"I – I am not certain if he would wish to see me."

"Of course he will." Lady Frederica tossed her head, her curls bouncing. "Let us go and see. If we cannot find him then, at the very least, we will be able to discover what has happened. I can assure you, he will not blame you in the least, Lady Alice."

With a nod, Alice pushed herself away from the wall and threaded her arm through Miss Fairley's.

"That is true." Pushing down the rest of her concern, she lifted her chin and prayed that everything her friends had said to reassure her would come true. No one would look at her, no one would whisper about her, no one would speak about what she had done to Lord Sedgewick... and Lord Sedgewick himself would not reject her. Courage took some moments but all the same, with her friends on either side of her, Alice found herself prepared enough to walk across the ballroom. "Come then, let us see if we can find Lord Sedgewick... and let us pray that he will be able to recover, just as he has done before."

CHAPTER TEN

"Again?"

Simon could only groan, clutching at his stomach with both hands as the physician, who had returned with great speed, attempted to examine him.

"This is impossible! How could you be struck down in the very same way only the day after you have recovered from the first injury?" Lord Larbert threw up his hands and began to pace up and down Simon's drawing room as though, somehow, that was going to be of help. "There does not seem to be any clear sense in this. Someone must be doing this to you - and doing it to you deliberately."

"I think I would concur, my Lord," the physician murmured, straightening before turning around to look through whatever concoctions he had in his bag. "Now, it is as before. You will have to drink this and thereafter, whatever is cast up will take the poison away from you."

There was nothing for it and though it was most

unpleasant, Simon did as bidden and, within a half hour, had returned to the drawing room to sit down in his chair.

The physician lifted an eyebrow.

"Is there much improvement?"

Beads of sweat broke out across Simon's forehead.

"Yes, some," he managed to press out through dry, cracked lips. "I do not feel in as much pain as before."

The physician nodded and stepped forward, one hand going to Simon's face.

"You are a little clammy and I would advise rest for the remainder of the evening and all day tomorrow."

"That is all?" Simon slowly loosened his hands from where he'd pressed them into his stomach. "There is nothing else that needs to be done?"

"Not that I can see." The physician lifted his shoulders and let them fall. "It is as both yourself and Lord Larbert have identified – it is the very same issue as the last time I came to examine you. Now that you have purged yourself, it will take a little time, but your recovery will be relatively swift, I am sure."

Simon closed his eyes and dropped his head back, resting it on the tall cushion of the couch, saying nothing.

"Do you have any advice as to what Lord Sedgewick could do to prevent further illness?"

Lord Larbert's tone sounded a little frustrated and Simon could not blame his friend for such a feeling. After all, the physician had offered very little advice, and that was not going to be at all helpful in the days going forward.

"Advice? What advice do you think I am able to offer a gentleman of such good standing as Lord Sedgewick? I have helped him recover, and that is all that is expected of me, surely?"

Simon looked at Lord Larbert.

"I suppose that is fair. After all, the good physician has told me that this came about most likely due to something I ate or drank." His eyes went to the physician. "I presume that consideration is still the same?" Seeing the physician nod, Simon held out his hands wide. "Then what is there for him to say, Larbert? The only advice I can be given, the only advice I can take, is to make certain that I do not eat or drink anything at any social occasion I attend."

"Which is ridiculous," Lord Larbert retorted, sharply. "You're going to be dying of thirst should you reach the end of a ball without ever taking a single sip of anything. And, no doubt, you will end up in weakness and malady from not eating."

"I can eat well enough, just not at soirees and the like." The more he spoke, the more Simon began to sense doubts rising up in him. "As for dinners... well, mayhap I ought to refuse to attend them."

"I shall take my leave." The physician bowed and then picked up his bag before backing toward the door. "I shall call again in the morning, my Lord, should you wish it."

"I will send for you if I feel there is need," Simon replied, deciding that he did not want the physician to be prodding at him again, not unless his malady became worse. "Thank you." Watching as the physician left the room, Simon turned and shook his head to Lord Larbert. "I do not know what you expected him to say."

"I wanted him to tell you what it was that has made you so unwell!" With a roll of his eyes, Lord Larbert began to pace again, just as he had done when the physician was present. "It is not at all specific."

Simon hesitated, aware that what Lord Larbert said was true, but finding that he did not feel the same irritation.

"He will not know what is served at balls and other social occasions."

"But this does mean that we believe, now, that someone is attempting to make you unwell."

With a scowl, Simon ran one hand over his chin and then closed his eyes.

"I think that is true, yes. I cannot deny that it is much too specific for it to be accidental."

"And you do not think that Lady Alice–"

"No!" Such was the force of his exclamation, Lord Larbert's eyes flared wide in surprise, but Simon did not pull himself back. "I was the one who embarrassed her this evening, for what is now the second time. I could not linger for a second longer during our waltz and was forced to step aside and leave her standing there alone! I ought to apologize to her, in fact." Seeing Lord Larbert's slight frown, he shook his head. "No, I will not think for a moment that Lady Alice has had anything to do with this. She does not need to, and has no desire to injure me! We have only just become properly acquainted."

Lord Larbert slowly began to nod, his brow furrowing all the more, however.

"That leaves us with a great deal to consider, then."

Simon frowned.

"In what way?"

"If you cannot think of even one single person who might have sought to do such a thing to you, then what is the solution? Must we consider *everyone* within society, until we settle on the person responsible?"

A great and vast chasm opened up at Simon's feet and he swallowed hard, glancing over the top of it and seeing nothing but darkness below. Lord Larbert was quite correct. There was very little that he could do or say to even begin to discover who might have done such a thing to him. After all, he did not have any particular enemies, and there was no one whom he had wronged recently – so who would have disliked him so strongly as to attempt to injure him so severely?

"I might suggest that someone could be jealous of your interest in Lady Alice but that does not make any sense either, given that she is a wallflower, and no one even sees her."

"Indeed," Simon murmured, his thoughts aligned with Lord Larbert's. Lady Alice had been dancing with him when, on two occasions, he had been taken violently ill, but both of those occasions had been the waltz – did that have something to do with it? Was it more that he had been stepping out for the waltz with a wallflower, rather than with someone else? Someone who might wish to dance the waltz with him? Letting out a groan, he rubbed one hand over his face. "It becomes more and more confusing the longer I think of it. I do not know what to make of it all." Dropping his hand, he looked straight at his friend. "But I must speak to Lady Alice tomorrow, provided that I am well enough to go to call upon her."

Lord Larbert's eyes grew large.

"You intend to call on the wallflower?"

"Yes, I do." Simon did not even hesitate. "I have much to reassure her about, I think, and I will not pull myself back from that, no matter what may be said of me."

"Much may be said of you," Lord Larbert warned. "The *ton* may say that you are pursuing the wallflower, that you have been dancing with her twice over and now seek to call on her! It *will* be noticed, Sedgewick."

There came not even the smallest flicker of concern in Simon's heart. Instead, he closed his eyes and leaned his head back, his determination settling within him.

"Regardless, that is my intention, and I shall go through with it without even a thought."

"Provided you can stand and walk without any pain or difficulty."

Cracking open one eye, Simon scowled as Lord Larbert grinned.

"Yes, provided that I can do such a thing without showing any weakness. The last thing I wish to do is collapse to the floor all over again."

"Especially when you have done so twice over," came the laughing reply, though Simon's scowl only grew. "Very well, if you are determined to go, then I shall come with you. Not because I wish to keep society's gaze from you, but just in case you require me."

Simon wanted to say that he had no qualms whatsoever when it came to stepping into his carriage and making his way to Lady Alice's townhouse but, given the weakness which was currently within his frame, he could not bring himself to speak those words. Instead, he gave a small nod, and soon found his eyelids growing heavy, the urge to drift off to sleep beginning to overtake him.

"I am sorry, but I must retire." Pushing himself up before he fell asleep in his chair, he begrudgingly accepted Lord Larbert's arm and used him to lean on to walk to the door, fatigue clinging to every part of him. "Thank you, Larbert."

"But of course. You have had me rather worried, you know," his friend replied, continuing to walk with Simon to the staircase and then up the staircase itself. "I am glad that you are not gravely ill."

Simon chuckled but, at the same time, appreciated all that his friend had said.

"As am I, Larbert. As am I."

∽

"Lady Alice, thank you for seeing me."

When he lifted his head, Simon could not help but smile at the young lady, taking in her wide eyes and the pink that had risen to her cheeks. Clearly, his visit had been something of a surprise, but thankfully, it did not seem to be unwelcome, given the smile edging across her lips.

"I am glad to see you recovered. Please, do sit down. You too, Lord Larbert."

"I thank you."

Doing as he was bidden, Simon sat down quickly,

glad that the strength of body he had found had lasted this long, though it was already beginning to weaken. There was a quiet tremor to his frame and, as he let out a breath of relief when he sat down, he caught the way that Lady Alice's eyes settled on his.

"You are still fatigued, I think."

"I am," he agreed, not at all embarrassed to admit it. "But I am not unwell, or in pain, and for that, I am grateful."

She nodded, rose, and rang the bell for tea, glancing at the maid who sat in the corner of the room, next to the open door.

"My mother will be sorry that she has missed you both. In fact, I am not certain that she will believe me when I tell her that not one, but two, gentlemen called upon me this morning!"

With a quiet laugh, she sat back down, and Simon could not help but smile at the sound. It was gentle, warming him through, and as he gazed back into her eyes, Simon's heart began to yearn for her closeness... and he did not push such feelings away.

"I wanted to reassure you that all was well," he said, quickly, "*and* to state that there is nothing about this for which I blame you. I do not think that this had anything to do with you, and I am truly sorry for having to step away from you as I did."

Lady Alice shook her head.

"Please, do not apologize. I understand that you had to remove yourself from the dance at once."

"But I left you standing there alone, and I am sorry

for that." With a shrug, he smiled at her. "It was unavoidable, but I would like to dance with you again."

Much to his surprise, instead of appearing at all pleased by this, Lady Alice's eyes flared, and she looked away.

"I – I am not certain that such a thing would be wise, Lord Sedgewick. After all, in the two instances where we have stood up together, you have been taken ill, and I must believe now that it is a deliberate act that has caused this."

The door opened, the tea tray was brought in and, as Lady Alice busied herself with that, Simon let himself study her. Her dark brown eyes had been filled with worry, her lips flat and her face a little pale when he had mentioned dancing with her again. Obviously, there was a great concern there, and it was not one which Simon wanted to ignore or brush off. However, he would not permit it to hold him back from stepping out with her again, so long as she could be convinced to agree.

"I thank you." When she set the tea down in front of him, Simon looked up at her. "I do not think that it is because of you that I have been taken ill, Lady Alice. I should not want you to think that."

Lady Alice bit her lip and set a cup and saucer down in front of Lord Larbert.

"I am not so certain, Lord Sedgewick. After all, I am a wallflower, with a father who is disgraced, and it is not expected for a gentleman such as you to stand up with someone like me. Mayhap they are warning you – or even punishing you – for dancing with me."

"I do not think it would be because of you."

Harrumphing, Lord Larbert spoke again and picked up his tea, his voice booming through the rest of the living room. "I have been considering it, as Lord Sedgewick has done also, and I am quite certain that the reason for this has nothing to do with you. I think that whoever stood up with Lord Sedgewick for those waltzes would have found themselves abandoned by him as he struggled against this strange malady placed upon him. I believe that someone is making quite certain that he cannot ever dance the waltz again."

Lady Alice blinked, her eyes rounding as she looked back to Simon.

"Is that so? Why would someone do that to you?"

Simon shook his head and sighed.

"I do not know. It is a struggle to even *think* about who it might be, for there are so many gentlemen and ladies within society and I confess, I do not have a grudge against anyone... though Lord Larbert believes that there is someone who holds something against me, however."

"And you do not know as to what it might be?"

With a grimace, Simon shook his head.

"It is all very confusing. I do not know what I have done or who I might have upset for there is nothing – to my mind at least – that I can recall doing to anyone! But it seems to me that there is a purpose behind my illness. The physician reminded me that it must have come in something that I ate or drank and–"

"The brandy!"

Simon paused, seeing the way that Lady Alice's eyes flared.

"I beg your pardon?"

"Do you not recall?" There was excitement in her face now, as she leaned forward in her chair. "The first time we were to dance together, the footman brought a tray to where we stood. I was upset, I admit, for he did not so much as glance at us, but instead offered it only to you."

"And there was only one glass upon it," Simon finished, remembering the moment precisely. "I took it and threw it back without hesitation."

"I do recall that you grimaced and, when I looked at you, believing that the scowl came from having to stand up with a wallflower, you stated that there was a foul taste to the brandy."

Letting out a slow breath, Simon turned his gaze to Lord Larbert, smiling tightly at Lord Larbert's wide eyes.

"Lady Alice, you have done me a great service," he murmured, pushing one hand through his hair, a tingling running through him as he recalled everything Lady Alice had described. "I had quite forgotten about the brandy."

She smiled, though it did not linger.

"Might I ask if you had any brandy last evening also?"

Simon nodded.

"Given that I believed my first bout of illness came about from an unfortunate circumstance and was not at all deliberate, I ate and drank quite freely last evening. Indeed, I think I had only finished my second brandy before we stepped out to dance."

"Then it *was* the brandy," Lord Larbert murmured, as Simon saw Lady Alice nod. "Someone placed something in your glass and, unwittingly, you drank it."

Silence flooded the room as each of them contemplated this new revelation, this bold understanding, and found themselves a little overwhelmed by it. Simon, whilst relieved that Lady Alice had shown him how such a thing might have occurred, did not have any further thoughts about *who* might have done such a thing and thus, he found himself still facing the vast chasm he had felt only a few minutes before.

"I will be of aid to you, if I can." Looking back at Lady Alice, he watched as her smile began to fade, perhaps due to not seeing what she had hoped for in his eyes. "I am aware that as a wallflower, my place is at the back of any ballroom, of any soiree, but mayhap I would still be able to do something to help you discover the truth."

"I would be grateful for all and any help, Lady Alice," Simon said quickly, his heart leaping when her smile returned. "You have been a wonderful support already and the truth is, I feel so very lost, I do not know what I ought to do next!"

"I am certain that we will find a way forward," she told him, the confidence shining in her eyes and the smile on her face giving him a small spark of hope. "Let us pray that, from this day on, you are not attacked by such a malady again."

"I will agree to that!" With a quiet laugh, Simon picked up his cup of tea and took a small sip, glad when it did not send any pain to his stomach. "Thank you, Lady Alice. I feel a little more confident already."

CHAPTER ELEVEN

"So what are you to do?"

Alice shook her head and sighed.

"I do not know. I was so happy when Lord Sedgewick accepted my offer of support in all of this, but it was only when he took his leave that I realized that I did not know what it was I could do!" Her shoulders lifted and then fell again as another heavy breath escaped from her. "I feel myself a little foolish now, for I do not know what it is I am meant to do."

Miss Fairley tilted her head, her eyes roving around the room as she considered.

"Mayhap you can simply be a wallflower."

A frown danced across Alice's forehead.

"What do you mean?"

"Wallflowers are excellent creatures when it comes to seeing everything but being able to do very little." Miss Fairley's eyebrow lifted. "Do you recall how we were able to tell you about all the various gentlemen at the first ball we attended together? We were able to warn you away from some of them and that is because we know of their reputation and have seen their behavior towards others. We have not experienced it ourselves, of course, but as wallflowers, all we do is watch and wait. Therefore, why not use such a thing to your advantage in this situation?"

Alice nodded slowly, letting the idea settle in her mind.

"I suppose I could do so."

"You might see more than you think," her friend encouraged. "Look, at this very moment, we see Lady Rachael and her sister, Lady Hannah, walking behind Lord Umbridge and Lord Delford. Can you see which of the two gentlemen they have their attention set on?"

Alice followed her friend's gaze and looked through the room, finally spying the two ladies. She noted with interest that neither of them was looking at Lord Delford, but rather they had their attention set on Lord Umbridge. Their heads were close together, murmuring quietly, but their eyes were fixed on Lord Umbridge's back.

"They seek Lord Umbridge's attention."

"Precisely. Now, do you think that they would share that with anyone in particular? No, they would not. They might tell a trusted friend, but at this moment, they do not want the *ton* to know of their interest, no doubt. And yet you and I are aware of it."

"I can see what you mean." A little more at ease now, Alice let her gaze run over the other gentlemen and ladies in the drawing room, taking each of them in. "Lord Chamberlain is looking toward Lady Hamilton a great deal, though he is already wed, is he not?"

Miss Fairley scowled.

"Yes, indeed he is."

"And Miss Mullins is laughing very prettily at something Lord Blackton has said," Alice continued, warming to the idea. "Do you truly think that I might be able to be of assistance to Lord Sedgewick in this way?"

"Of course I do." With a warm smile, Miss Fairley turned to look back at her, rather than study the room any further. "You think well of him, do you not?"

Alice did not even pretend to hide her interest.

"I think him a wonderful gentleman."

Miss Fairley smiled, her expression softening.

"That is good. He is not a gentleman with a poor reputation, nor someone who has any sort of concern over his behavior. In fact, did he not protect you from Lord Cartwright?"

"He did." Her heart spun in her chest. "That would be a gentleman whom Lord Sedgewick might consider, as someone who would dislike him, would it not?"

"Lord Cartwright?" Miss Fairley bit her lip, then nodded. "Yes, I think that would be a wise consideration. I am surprised that he has not thought about him before!"

"I think that this has all been so very unexpected that he cannot think clearly of anything much at the moment."

Alice swallowed quickly, aware of how her heart began to pound at the thought of Lord Sedgewick. When he had come to call on her, she had been so startled that it had taken her a few minutes to feel anything but surprise. Now, however, those warm feelings she had only just admitted to herself were beginning to grow with such speed that Alice was certain they would soon overtake her entirely.

"That is understandable, but you must suggest Lord Cartwright to him. Surely that would make sense, given what took place between them?" A smile darted across Miss Fairley's lips. "Mayhap this is not going to be as difficult as you both fear."

"Mayhap." Taking a deep breath, Alice set her shoulders and lifted her chin. "But I shall remain watchful nonetheless."

"You need not watch for me, Lady Alice, for I am already present." With a start, Alice turned around, only to smile as Lord Sedgewick himself bowed towards her, a grin flashing across his face. "Forgive me, I did not mean to startle you."

"It is quite all right," Alice replied, aware of how her heart pounded at the sight of him standing so close to her again. "You must be much improved, Lord Sedgewick, which I am very glad to see."

"Thank you, I am. In fact, in the two days we have been absent from each other, I find myself back to my usual strength." A warmth came into his blue eyes and Alice had to stop herself from reaching out to touch him, a fierce desire to be closer to him burning right through her. "Should you like to walk with me, Lady Alice?"

Her smile froze on her face.

"Walk with you?"

"Yes. It is a soiree, and there is not too much going on, other than conversation and the like, so why should we not step out together? Miss Fairley, should you like to join us?"

"I must," came the reply, "given that I will act as chaperone."

"My mother is resting," Alice said, quickly. "She is present, but sitting down for the moment. I believe that she finds soirees a little more intimidating than balls, for it is all the more obvious when people do not speak to her."

A dark look passed across Lord Sedgewick's face, chasing away his smile.

"That is disappointing to hear, Lady Alice. I am sorry for it."

"She is contented enough."

With a nod, he turned his head away, his jaw working furiously for a few moments before finally, he looked back at her again.

"Very well. Then would you like to walk with me through the house? The parlor, library and gardens are open to guests, and it would be much better than standing here and conversing!"

Alice blinked, nervousness beginning to rush through her.

"You wish to walk with me?"

"Yes, of course I do." Lord Sedgewick laughed lightly and even Miss Fairley joined in with him. "That is why I asked you." The laughter in his face began to disappear. "However, if you do not wish to walk with me, then I quite understand."

"No, no, I would be glad to do so, truly!" Alice began to stammer, her face flushing with embarrassment. "It is only that I am still a wallflower and–"

"You are not a wallflower to me, not any longer."

Without warning, Lord Sedgewick stepped forward and his hand went to hers. "I do not see you in that light."

Tears began to burn behind her eyes, but Alice blinked them away rapidly.

"The *ton* may speak of it."

"Yes, they might. But I do not think that I care very much about what the *ton* should say in this matter."

There was nothing else for her to say, no other worry for her to voice. Lord Sedgewick had taken all of them and thrown them asunder, leaving her with only one choice – to accept him. Glancing to Miss Fairley, who smiled encouragingly, Alice forced a smile to her lips, still feeling a little uncertain and wondering just who from the *ton* would be the first to notice them.

"Thank you, Lord Sedgewick. I think that I would be glad to accept."

"Capital." With a broad smile, he offered her his arm, and a little tentatively, Alice took it, aware of the strength that ran underneath her fingers. Fear began to bite down hard but she ignored it, keeping her gaze straight ahead rather than looking into the faces of any of the other guests. "I have been thinking about you."

Alice's head twisted sharply, looking up at Lord Sedgewick with surprise.

"I think that my gratitude for your consideration of me, as well as your wisdom, knows no bounds," he continued, not glancing towards her at all. "It was you who realized that the brandy I had taken held whatever poison it was that ailed me so. Rather than be upset or embarrassed for your own sake – for being left in the middle of the dance floor without a partner must have been extremely trying – you cared enough about my wellbeing to come to call upon me the first time."

"And I would have done so again the second time, had you not called first." Seeing him smile at her, she blushed. "I mean only to say that I was eager to know that you were recovered."

"I have recovered entirely and must hope not to be injured so again!" A tug at his lips set a darker look upon Lord Sedgewick's expression. "I will have to stay away from brandy and the like at whatever social occasion I attend."

"Might I ask if Lord Cartwright could be involved?"

"Lord Cartwright?" Lord Sedgewick glanced at her. "I suppose that he should have been the first person I thought of! I cannot say why I forgot about him. Of course, he should be the very first person I should think of!"

"Though it may be a little obvious."

Lord Sedgewick chuckled rather ruefully.

"Yes, I suppose it might be, but then again, Lord Cartwright has never been one to be discreet."

Recalling how he had attempted to force her to do as he wished, a slight tremble ran over Alice's frame.

"That is true. What shall you do about him?"

"I shall ask him." Lord Sedgewick shrugged one shoulder. "What else is there to be done? I shall simply ask him directly if he is attempting to injure me, as retaliation for what I did to him, and will see what it is he has to say for himself."

Worry spiked in Alice's heart.

"What if he refuses to say anything? What if he denies it outright?"

"Then I shall continue to consider who might be doing such a thing and why." The smile on Lord Sedgewick's face was not wry any longer. "And in the meantime, I shall make certain not to eat or drink anything at any social occasions unless I have no other choice."

"That will make you very uncomfortable at times, I am sure. There must be something else you can do. Mayhap Lord Larbert would be able to take a drink for himself but instead, offer it to you? You cannot remain starved and thirsty throughout the rest of the Season!"

Lord Sedgewick chuckled.

"Mayhap but –"

"Good evening, Lord Sedgewick."

Alice, noticing how quickly she was ignored, immediately made to step back but Lord Sedgewick, much to her surprise, pulled his arm close to his body so that she could not take her hand from where it rested.

"Lady Helen, good evening," he replied, gesturing to Alice. "Are you acquainted with Lady Alice?"

Looking into the young lady's face, which wore a rather sharp expression, Alice forced a smile to her lips which she did not truly feel. It was clear from the look on Lady Helen's face that she did not appreciate Alice's presence and perhaps thought that Lord Sedgewick ought not to be walking with her.

"We are acquainted, yes."

Alice spoke first, her voice almost steady.

Still being careful not to look at her, Lady Helen

sniffed lightly and turned her head away completely, almost giving Alice the cut direct. Her voice, when she spoke, had a hard edge to it.

"Some time ago, I think."

"Yes, from last Season," Alice answered quickly, recalling that Lady Helen had been an acquaintance from the previous year, *before* the scandal about her father had been spread throughout London. "How nice to speak with you again."

"I wish I could say the same," came the sharp reply. "Lord Sedgewick, surely you must have heard about Lady Alice's father and his wrongdoings? Why, then, should you wish to walk with her? I should very much like to be in your company."

Under her hand, Alice felt Lord Sedgewick's arm tighten, though when he spoke, his voice was quiet and calm.

"Forgive me, Lady Helen, but I do not think that anyone should bear the blame for the wrongdoings of others, even if it is one's father or mother."

Lady Helen blinked and, as Alice watched, stretched a wide smile across her face rather than a frown. It was not directed at her, however, but instead, sent in Lord Sedgewick's direction.

"You are such a generous gentleman, Lord Sedgewick. Your heart is kind, and I am humbled by that. Come, shall we walk in the gardens together? I am certain that Lady Alice will not mind waiting back here." She flashed another sharp look towards Alice. "After all, I am sure that you are used to waiting in the shadows, Lady Alice."

The pain which such a remark brought was more than Alice had expected, and though she nodded and tried to smile, it shot through her and she pulled her hand away from Lord Sedgewick's arm at once.

"But of course."

Mumbling, she turned around and made to leave, only for another gentleman to walk directly into her. At the same time, Lord Sedgewick let out such a loud exclamation that almost everyone's attention was brought towards him, Alice's included.

"Goodness, Lady Helen, there is no need for Lady Alice to step away!" Lord Sedgewick declared, sounding both firm and amiable at the same time. "We can walk together, the three of us."

Alice swallowed hard, wanting to tell him that he did not need to show her such consideration, and that he was bringing a good deal of attention to himself, because of his taking this stance, but the words caught in her throat, and she could not bring herself to say even a single word.

"I hardly think that you need to walk with Lord Sedgewick, Lady Helen." The gentleman who had knocked into Alice, the one who now stood between her and Lord Sedgewick, interrupted what Lord Sedgewick had been saying, speaking directly to the lady instead. "I have been waiting for some time for your company and if Lord Sedgewick is determined to be in company with a wallflower rather than with you alone, then that is *his* failing and foolishness, is it not? Come, I will walk with you in the gardens."

Lady Helen laughed gaily and though Alice stepped

back, taking herself away from the conversation, she could not help but hear it regardless.

"You are very kind, Lord Westerly. How generous of you to step in. Lord Sedgewick, can you not see that your wallflower has done as I have asked her, however? There can be no reason for us not to walk together now."

"Mayhap I can take Lady Alice's place."

The words came from another young lady, who had just approached, and Alice looked on in confusion, unable to clearly see the newcomer's face from where she stood.

"Whatever is going on?"

A light touch to Alice's shoulder made her flinch, though relief poured into her as Lady Frederica came to stand beside her, watching the scene unfolding before them.

"Lady Helen asked Lord Sedgewick to walk with her and sent me away from him. Lord Sedgewick told her that we could all walk together but then another gentleman came to her and said that *he* would go in Lord Sedgewick's place, since Lord Sedgewick did not want to give up his conversation with me." Alice put one hand to her forehead, letting out a slow breath. "I am glad that I stepped away when I did. Now, however, another young lady is approaching, who has just said that she will take my place, so that Lord Sedgewick, Lady Helen, and herself might walk together."

"Goodness." Lady Frederica blinked. "I am aware that a Marquess seeking a bride is an opportunity for almost every young lady in London to push themselves forward, but I did not think that some would be quite this brazen!"

Alice frowned, her heart twisting in her chest.

"Do you think that is what Lady Helen and whoever the other lady is–"

"Lady Christina."

"What Lady Helen and Lady Christina are hoping for? That he might think of one of them?"

Lady Frederica nodded.

"I should think so. After all, Lord Sedgewick is a Marquess, rich and handsome. He has certainly become a little more involved in society this Season and thus, there will be the hope that he has decided to settle on a wife."

The way that her heart fell to the floor and shattered had Alice looking away, a desperate sadness coursing through her. It was foolish to let herself think that the Marquess would ever consider someone such as her, even though, at this present moment, there was certainly a connection between them.

But not a connection that could ever grow to anything more than what it is at present. We are acquainted, yes, but I cannot let myself hope for a furthering of that, especially not into anything profound.

"He is looking at you."

Alice lifted her head and gazed directly back into Lord Sedgewick's face. His jaw was set, his eyes suddenly dark and flashing but the anger within his expression was not directed towards her, given the way that his eyes darted from one person to the next, only to then meet hers again.

"Mayhap you should join him again."

With a small shake of her head, Alice looked away.

"I do not think that I can, not when there are three others already in discussion with him. I fear that my presence might make the situation even more difficult."

"I think that he wishes for you to return to his side."

It was a hope that Alice felt burning in her heart, but she refused to give way to it.

"I do not think that he hopes for that at all. Most likely, he wishes that the conversation between the two ladies and Lord Westerly will come to an end very soon!"

Lady Frederica looked at her, a sad smile on her face.

"You will not have even a little hope?"

"I cannot."

With these words, Alice turned away directly and walked back across the room until she came to the door. Stepping through it without so much as a backward glance, Alice did not recognize the tears burning in her eyes until she was standing in the corner of the parlor, away from every other guest and now entirely alone. Given that no one paid her even the smallest bit of attention, she dropped her head and, after a moment, let her tears fall, catching them in her handkerchief. It was not the sadness of being a wallflower that brought such an agony to her heart but rather the realization that out of Lady Helen, Lady Christina, and herself, she was the least likely to find herself beside Lord Sedgewick. Yes, he had been kind and more than generous to her, but that was all she could expect from him, even if it brought her heart more agony than she had ever expected.

CHAPTER TWELVE

It had not been a pleasant evening and thus far, Simon was rather frustrated. Having been quite enjoying the company of Lady Alice, he had then been interrupted by Lady Helen, who had seemed determined to insult Lady Alice for no other reason than she clearly considered her lesser than her, and thereafter, both Lord Westerly and Lady Christina had come to join the fray. It had taken all of his strength to remain where he was and not go chasing after Lady Alice, who had taken her leave of the group, once the discussion had become a little stronger. He had despised Lady Helen for her insults but, of course, had been unable to say anything of the sort given that they were in company. Thus, he had been forced to walk about with Lady Helen, Lady Christina, *and* Lord Westerly, listening to them speak about all manner of banal things while his thoughts had lingered upon Lady Alice, wondering now how she was feeling, and praying that she would allow him back into her company again. He could not imagine what it had been like for her to be pushed back in such a rude and unthinking manner, when she ought to be standing directly by him and with the other ladies, given her rank and standing. How he hoped she could understand that his desire had been for her company, *and* for her to return to the group! When he had looked at her, he had seen nothing but sadness in her eyes, though he had been very glad indeed to see that Lady Frederica had been standing with her.

At least she was not alone.

"What say you, Lord Sedgewick?"

Simon harrumphed, looking about the group and taking in Lord Westerly's frown and Lady Christina's hopeful eyes before turning his attention to Lady Helen.

"I – I think it an excellent notion."

In truth, he had very little idea as to what they were speaking of, but he could not say that he had been ignoring the conversation as much as he could and therefore, had no knowledge of their topic of choice. His gamble seemed to work well for Lady Christina beamed at him and Lady Helen's expression lit up with a smile. It was only Lord Westerly who appeared displeased but, then again, he always appeared to be so when Simon was in his company. A swirling through his stomach only intensified as Lady Helen grasped his arm and pulled him towards the door, making him wonder precisely what it was he had agreed to and why, then, he was being taken in the entirely opposite direction from where he wished to go.

"It is decided, Mama!"

Much to Simon's surprise, they came to a stop

directly beside Lady Williamson who turned her eyes first to her daughter and, thereafter, to Lord Westerly, then Lady Christina and then to Simon himself.

"Good evening to you all." With a small, indulgent smile, she looked at her daughter. "What is it that you are saying, my dear?"

"Lord Sedgewick thinks that a Masquerade Ball is a capital idea and has agreed to host it at his townhouse!" Lady Helen's excited exclamations had Simon's stomach lurching in surprise, and he opened his mouth to say something, only to snap it closed as he remembered what he had said to her, not realizing what she had been speaking of. His words had been an acceptance of her suggested idea, and he could not deny them now. "It will have to be a very few select guests, of course but I am more than willing to assist you with that, Lord Sedgewick."

"As am I, of course." Lady Christina put one hand to his arm. "You will dance with me, will you not? You will be wearing a mask, I know, but I will be certain to find you out long before the evening comes to an end!"

Simon blinked and mumbled something, though he made certain not to agree to Lady Christina's expectations. Lady Williamson looked at him and smiled, her eyes holding the same vivid intensity as her daughter's.

"How wonderful, Lord Sedgewick! That is very kind of you indeed. I know that my daughter would be thrilled to attend as your guest. How generous of you."

"But of course." Clearing his throat, Simon inclined his head. "I will make all of the arrangements. The invitations will come out in due course."

He went to turn away, only for Lady Helen to grasp at his arm.

"Wait a moment." Pouting, she tilted her head. "You do not wish me to aid you with this? I have only just stated that I will assist you with the invitations for, to my mind, those who are to be invited should be very carefully selected. After all, Lord Sedgewick," she continued, a light smile on her lips as she took a step closer, one hand still on his arm as her voice softened, "you are the *Marquess* of Sedgewick which is, indeed, a very high title. You should be surrounded by only the very best of society."

Anger burned a fire up Simon's chest and into his eyes and he quickly pulled his arm back, lifting his chin a little as he did so.

"Though I appreciate your willingness to be of aid, Lady Helen, and yours also, Lady Christina, I will not require your assistance. Now, if you will excuse me."

Fully aware that he was being a little rude, but also seeing that Lady Helen wished to be certain that only those *she* deemed fit would attend his ball – which was certainly not the likes of Lady Alice – Simon stepped away before he exploded into a fit of rage. Lady Helen was not only forward, she was overbearing, and her cruel words and hard response to Lady Alice made him less than willing to spend any more time in her company.

"You look a little upset."

Simon rolled his eyes and said nothing as his friend fell into step with him.

"Are you going somewhere in particular?"

"To the drawing room. I thought Lady Alice –"

"She is in the gardens with her friends."

Simon stopped and turned sharply, leaving Lord Larbert to follow him.

"Whatever is the matter, old boy?" Lord Larbert put one hand on Simon's shoulder, forcing him to slow his steps. "You are walking through here as though you are a fierce wind, determined to blow wherever it pleases. What has troubled you so?"

"Aside from promising to hold a Masquerade Ball at my townhouse, on both Lady Helen and Lady Christina's request – though I did not know that was what they were asking until I had already agreed to it – I have had to endure Lady Helen's spiteful remarks as regards Lady Alice, *and* I have seen her attempting to make certain that all wallflowers are not able to attend this Masquerade Ball!"

Lord Larbert blinked and took a small step away, as though Simon's tirade had pushed him backwards. Simon blew out a breath, realizing that he had been rather direct in his speech though, in speaking as he had done, some of the strain had gone from him, his chest loosening just a little.

"I see." Lord Larbert cleared his throat, then began to smile. "Though mayhap you ought to be grateful for this opportunity to host such a ball?"

Simon grimaced.

"Why ever should I be glad of such a thing? I did not *want* to host a ball and certainly not at Lady Helen's request!"

"Because," Lord Larbert pointed out, his smile growing to a grin, "at a Masquerade, no one knows who anyone else is. Why not invite Lady Alice *and* all of her friends? They will be able to dance and smile and enjoy the evening just as any other young lady might. Mayhap Lady Alice with thank you for such an idea and then you will find yourself quite delighted, I am sure." The idea began to settle into Simon's mind and his anger fizzled away almost completely as Lord Larbert began to chuckle. "You see? It is not as bad as you feared!" his friend exclaimed, as Simon began to grin. "It is an excellent notion, I think, even if you entered into it unwittingly *and* unwillingly."

"Mayhap you are right," Simon mused slowly, as Lord Larbert laughed again. "I think that..."

He came to a sudden stop as his gaze suddenly found itself settling on none other than Lord Cartwright. Seeing the sternness of his gaze, Lord Larbert turned to look and then immediately let out a low growl.

"I see Lord Cartwright is present. Well, he is best left alone. After all, he–"

"What if *he* is the one attempting to injure me?"

"What do you mean?"

Quickly, Simon explained what Lady Alice had suggested, only for Lord Larbert's eyes to round as he too came to the same conclusion as Simon: Lord Cartwright ought to have been the very first person they considered and yet, for some reason, they had chosen not to do so.

"And you think to confront him?" Lowering his voice, Lord Larbert frowned and took a step closer to Simon. "Now? In the middle of a soiree?"

"Why should I not?" Simon asked, sidestepping his friend, and making his way across the floor. The anger that he had dampened down began to come to him with a greater strength, and he curled his hands into fists, ready now to speak to Lord Cartwright, to demand to know what it was that he had been trying to do to him. "Cartwright." With a lip already curling, Simon drew himself up as Lord Cartwright threw him an equally ugly look. "I want to speak with you." Tossing a sharp look to Lord Steelforth, who had been speaking with Lord Cartwright, Simon jerked his head to the left, indicating that the man should step away and, after a moment, Lord Steelforth did so without even a single murmur of protest.

"If you are to tell me that I must stay away from *every* wallflower, then you need not do so." Lord Cartwright rubbed at his chin absentmindedly, as if he were remembering where Simon had struck him. "I have nothing I wish to say to you, Sedgewick. Be on your way. Many others would be glad of your company."

"No doubt you would be glad if I was gone from London," Simon stated, making no attempt to step away from Lord Cartwright, aware that the man's face was going a dull shade of red. "If I was gone for good, mayhap?"

A line drew down between Lord Cartwright's eyebrows.

"I do not much like that you planted me a facer, if that is what you mean. I should like to be able to go about my business – and seek out my desires – where I please and without being interrupted."

Simon snorted.

"Even if you are being pushed away?" Choosing not

to follow that particular focus, he shook his head. "I want to know if I am to hold you responsible, Cartwright. It seems most likely to be you and I would prefer that you spoke the truth to me on the subject."

Lord Cartwright's frown only deepened.

"Whatever are you talking about?"

"I think you know *precisely* what it is that I am speaking about."

"Then in that case, you are mistaken." A hint of steel came into Lord Cartwright's eyes as they narrowed. "If you are accusing me of something, then I should prefer to know precisely what it is, rather than attempting to guess."

Fire zipped up Simon's spine and he took a small step closer, all too aware of Lord Larbert's restraining presence beside him.

"My illness, Cartwright. My malady? It comes from nothing, appears with great strength, and then goes from me once the physician has visited. Apparently, it comes on from something I have eaten or drunk which means that *someone* is attempting to injure me deliberately."

"He nearly collapsed in the middle of a dance, such was the strength of it," Lord Larbert interjected. "Someone wished Lord Sedgewick to suffer a great deal of pain and trouble."

"And you think that I have done this?" Lord Cartwright shook his head and grimaced. "I have done no such thing. If I wanted to injure you in retaliation for what you have done to me, I should be bold enough to do it publicly – or at the very least, to make it clear that it was *I* who had done so. Why would I hide it from you?"

The anger that Simon had held within him, anger stemming from the belief that Lord Cartwright might well be responsible, began to die away. Lord Cartwright was a gentleman who had no qualms about acting in an inappropriate manner and was arrogant enough to make his revenge obvious.

"You see, now?" Lord Cartwright sneered, his disdain more than apparent. "You realize now that I am *not* the person you are seeking – though when you do find out who they are, I should like it very much if you would inform me as to who they are."

"And why should he do that?" Lord Larbert asked, only for Lord Cartwright to laugh darkly.

"Why, so that I might shake their hand!" came the response, making Simon's heart pound furiously as his anger returned. "I had been thinking of doing something as regarded your insult towards me, taking me from a young lady who no one else would have taken note of, but I think that this sounds as though it would be punishment enough! I only wish you had fallen to the floor and been trampled by the other dancers."

Fury surged in Simon's veins, and he made to step forward, only for Lord Larbert to put one hand on his arm, pulling him back. With a dark scowl, Simon turned on his heel and strode away, hearing Lord Cartwright's cackling laugh chasing after him.

"*Not* Lord Cartwright, then." Lord Larbert, who had already released Simon's arm, gave him a wry look. "I believe him. I assume you do too?"

"Yes, I do." As much as he did not wish to, Simon had to admit that there was truth in what he had seen in Lord

Cartwright's face, *and* heard him say. "I think he is too prideful to speak with any falsehood, and I do believe him when he says that, should he have taken revenge, he would wish me to know that it was him."

Lord Larbert let out a frustrated breath.

"Then I fear that this leaves us even more confused than before. Lord Cartwright seemed to be such an obvious fellow. If it is not he, then who else might it be?"

Simon rubbed one hand down his face, shaking his head as he dropped his hand.

"As much as I wish I could give you an answer, I am afraid that I cannot." With a scowl, he looked around the room, wondering if anyone present was the one responsible. "I must face the difficult truth of it all. Yet again, I am lost in confusion and uncertainty. I do not know – nor do I have even the smallest idea –who might have poisoned me."

CHAPTER THIRTEEN

"There you are!"

Alice looked up in surprise at the fervency within the voice of whoever it was speaking, only to smile into the face of Lord Sedgewick.

"Lord Sedgewick, good evening."

"I looked for you at the soiree, but I could not find you." Reaching out, he grasped her hand and then bowed over it. Lifting his head, he looked straight back at her. "I am sorry for what Lady Helen said, *and* for my lack of action thereafter. I should have immediately left the conversation and come in search of you."

Her heart immediately softened.

"I quite understand. You were being pulled into a conversation with others who were clearly interested in your company – and not particularly eager for mine." A slightly rueful note entered her voice and she looked away. "There is nothing for you to apologize for."

"I believe that there is." His hand tightened on hers,

seemingly eager to hold it a little longer rather than release it as he ought. "You *will* dance with me this evening, will you not?"

A flurry of surprise ran around Alice's stomach, and she caught her breath, looking back into his eyes and seeing him smile.

"You – you wish to stand up with me again, even though on the two previous occasions, you have been unwell because of it?"

Lord Sedgewick chuckled.

"It is a risk that I am willing to take, Lady Alice. Besides which, my card is beginning to fill, and I should like to make certain that I have your name written there amongst them." His smile grew a little weary. "I have already had Lady Helen and Lady Christina seek me out so that I might have no other choice but to sign their dance cards, even though I am not particularly enamored of the thought. I should very much like to dance with you, Lady Alice, so I might have some joy this evening. What say you?"

There was not even a momentary hesitation as she gave him her dance card, knowing that there would be no one else's name written there but feeling no shame over that. His words had brought her enough joy already.

"Thank you, Lord Sedgewick. That would make me very glad also."

Smiling, he took it from her and then dropped his head, writing his name and then handing the card back to her.

"I have something else I wish to tell you about. Lady

Helen – though rather direct and much too forward – managed to arrange for me to hold a Masquerade Ball. Initially I was rather frustrated, only for Lord Larbert to show me how excellent an idea it might be."

Alice tilted her head a little.

"Oh?"

"Because I shall be able to invite whomever I please and, of course, I have every intention of inviting you and all of your friends. Would that not be wonderful? An opportunity to dance, to laugh, and to be part of society without anything holding you back? No one would know who you were, given that everybody will be masked and therefore–"

"Oh, what a wonderful notion!" Before Lord Sedgewick had finished speaking, Alice had been overtaken by such a happiness and joy that she clapped her hands together in excitement, her whole being suddenly flooded with delight. "Lord Sedgewick, I do not know how I can thank you! The thought of being in amongst society as I was before, last Season, is so wonderful that it is almost too much for me to think of! To know that no one will look down at me with any degree of disdain is more wonderful than I think I can express!"

"I am delighted to see your happiness. Indeed, it fills my own heart with joy also." Lord Sedgewick grinned and, as a footman came close to him, a tray in his hand, he reached out and took the only brandy remaining. "How wonderful an evening it shall be!"

So saying, he took a sip – and, suddenly, all of Alice's happiness ripped away from her.

"Stop!"

Swallowing, Lord Sedgewick blinked at her.

"What in heavens name... oh!"

"The footman!"

Turning, Alice began to weave her way through the crowd of guests, seeking out the footman who had come so close to Lord Sedgewick in the knowledge that he would see the brandy and might very well take it. Seeing the man only a few paces away, she reached to grasp his arm, only for the footman to turn and for her eyes to go to the tray which held a great number of glasses.

It is not the same footman.

With a groan, Alice closed her eyes and dropped her head, just as Lord Sedgewick came to stand by her.

"That footman, was he-?"

"It was not the same footman." Alice opened her eyes. "I thought if I caught him, then I might be able to ask – nay, *demand* to know who had told him to take the brandy towards you but alas, I have not found the right person."

"And I have taken a little of that brandy." Lord Sedgewick's voice was low, and he rubbed one hand over his face. "I must now expect to become violently ill."

Alice shook her head.

"You only took a small amount. Let us hope that it was not enough to make you unwell... if it had anything in it at all." Her smile became a little wry. "I may have prevented you from taking the rest without any real need! Mayhap it is perfectly all right."

Lord Sedgewick shook his head.

"I do not think that it would have been. I have a

suspicion that the footman was sent towards me with the clear understanding that he make certain that I took the drink he offered, although I will not think poorly of the footman himself. It is not as though I suspect *him* of doing anything wrong, only of doing as he was bade."

"Of course." Alice gave him a small smile. "I do hope that you are not taken ill. I should be very sorry to miss my dance with you."

Lord Sedgewick's eyes flared.

"My dance! Good gracious, I must go to find Lady Helen at once!" He turned sharply, only to hurry back to her and grasp her hand, his eyes looking into hers. "Forgive me for stepping away in such haste, Lady Alice. I will return to you, I promise you."

He was gone the very next moment, leaving Alice with no opportunity to say anything to him. All the same, a smile spread right across her face as she turned away, ready to make her way back to the corner of the room now that Lord Sedgewick was gone. She did not feel at all frustrated or upset by his departure but rather found herself smiling, glad that he had thought to speak to her with such fervor and obvious interest, promising to return to her side just as soon as he was able. When was it that they had become so closely acquainted? She could not quite say, for the connection had been formed so slowly, but with such obvious strength that it was only now that she felt the full weight of it.

"What is it you think you are doing?"

Alice lifted her head and, a little surprised, looked back into the face of a young woman she was not acquainted with.

"I beg your pardon, but are you speaking with me?"

The young woman reached out and grasped Alice's arm, dragging her closer as her eyes spat fire.

"Of course I am speaking to you. Who else would it be?"

Her fingers tightened all the more, and Alice let out a yelp of pain, unable to pull back, such was the furious strength in the young woman's arm.

"Release me!"

Trying to pull herself out of the woman's grasp, she jerked her arm away, but the young woman held on tightly, her eyes narrowing all the more. Alice glanced around, her breathing coming in short, sharp gasps, but there was no one who could help her, given that she was already at the very edge of the ballroom. Who would look over at her? Who would care to even glance over at the shadows?

"I warn you now, stay away from Lord Sedgewick." The hiss of anger from the young lady's mouth had surprise leaping in Alice's heart, though she could only blink, words stuck in her throat. "He is a Marquess and you, only a shadow. What right have you to take up so much of his time? He–"

"I am the daughter of an Earl." Her courage had nearly failed her, but despite her pounding heart and churning stomach, Alice forced the words from her lips, seeing how the young woman's face went quite pale though her eyes were still sparkling with clear fury. "I have as much right to be in Lord Sedgewick's company as you do."

"*I* do not have a disgraced father," hissed the young

woman, her hand clamped on Alice's arm as she gave her a slight shake, though Alice tried, once more, to pull herself free. "Are you truly contented for Lord Sedgewick to tarnish his own reputation? That is certainly going to occur should he continue to seek out your company as he does at present. You are selfish indeed if that is so!"

"I think you should remove your hand from Lady Alice's arm, unless you wish your own reputation to be tarnished."

A little frantic, Alice looked over her shoulder, only to see Lady Frederica and Miss Fairley standing together, their faces set in expressions of obvious anger.

"How dare you place your hands on the daughter of an Earl?" Lady Frederica strode forward and made to physically pull the young woman's hand from Alice's arm though, much to Alice's relief, the young woman released her and stepped away a little before she could do so. Immediately rubbing her arm where the young woman's hand had been, Alice stepped back as Miss Fairley came to stand beside her. "What in heavens name do you think you are doing, Lady Christina?"

Lady Christina? Had she not been the other young lady who had joined Lady Helen and Lord Westerly, to push Alice away from Lord Sedgewick? She had, Alice was sure of it.

Quickly, Alice recalled how Lord Sedgewick had talked about Lady Christina earlier that very evening. Was she one of the young ladies he was to dance with? Why then had she come to speak to Alice in such a sharp and forward manner?

"I am reminding Lady Alice of her place." Lady

Christina lifted her chin, her jaw tight. "Do I mayhap need to remind you also?"

"You have nothing to say as regards our standing." Miss Fairley spoke up now, taking a step closer to Lady Christina. "We are just as you are. We have done nothing worthy of such disdain. Our behavior has been impeccable – though I could not say the same for you!"

"How dare you!" Lady Christina went bright red in the face, her eyes shining with such an obvious fury, Alice caught her breath in surprise, her arm still aching from where the lady had grasped it. "Wallflowers should not *dare* to speak in such a manner! I–"

"We speak as we please," Alice interrupted, though her voice wavered a little, "just as you do."

Lady Christina fell silent, her eyes going from Alice to Lady Frederica and then back to Miss Fairley. Her hands curled tightly, but she did not say a single word for some minutes, leaving them all to stand in silence. Alice wondered if she was expecting one of them to say something, perhaps even to apologize for speaking so, but they remained steadfast, saying nothing, but allowing the lady to simmer in her own upset.

"You have heard what I have said, Lady Alice." Eventually, Lady Christina broke the silence, her eyes narrowing again. "Stay away from Lord Sedgewick. He is not yours to take."

Seeing the lady about to turn away, Alice drew in a breath and, despite the shaking in her soul, spoke with a fierceness that she did not truly feel.

"I shall do as I please, Lady Christina. Your demands upon me shall have no effect whatsoever for I shall continue to spend as much time in his company as both he *and* I wish."

Lady Christina stamped her foot hard on the floor, her hands both curled up tightly into fists and she opened her mouth to say something, to respond with the same harshness, no doubt, only to grit her teeth, let out an exclamation of anger and turn to storm away.

Alice let out a slow breath and closed her eyes.

"Goodness, that was dreadful."

"It was." Miss Fairley put a hand to Alice's back. "Are you quite all right? I am sorry that we did not reach you more quickly. I–"

"What did you do to Lady Christina?"

Alice opened her eyes and shook her head. *Yet another person shouting at me?*

"I have done nothing to Lady Christina, my Lord."

"You have!" The gentleman was tall and thin with a long nose and dark eyes which were now solely fixed on Alice. "She is upset! She will not speak to me of it and–"

"And I have done nothing!" Alice interrupted, growing angry herself, now, at being spoken to in such a manner. "Lady Christina can make as many demands of me as she wishes, but I have no interest in complying with such demands – and if that displeases her, then so be it. Now, kindly remove yourself from my presence, for I certainly do not wish to stand here and have another prolonged argument over my behavior and what it is that I choose to do. I shall be in company with whomever I wish, I shall not pull back from Lord Sedgewick simply because Lady Christina wishes it, and I certainly shall not make any apology for stating so to Lady Christina. Good evening, my Lord."

Lifting her chin, she looked at the gentleman with a steady gaze, seeing how his face fell, his cheeks losing the color which they had held a few minutes beforehand. His shoulders rounded and he immediately began to frown as though something she had said displeased him a great deal.

"Lady Christina spoke of Lord Sedgewick?"

The quietness of his voice was in sharp contrast to the hard, unrelenting tone he had spoken with earlier and Alice blinked, a little taken aback by the sudden change.

"Yes, my Lord," she replied, speaking slowly as the gentleman's eyebrows fell low over his eyes. "She wished me to stay away from him."

"I see."

Without saying another word, the gentleman turned around and began to walk away from the three of them, leaving Alice to stare after him with such confusion in her heart that it was all she could do not to go after him and ask to know why he now appeared so despondent. With a shake of her head, she looked first to Lady Frederica and then to Miss Fairley, who both came to stand with her so that they might speak together.

"How very strange that was."

"That is none other than Lord Steelforth," Lady Frederica murmured, looking after the gentleman. "I am surprised that he spoke to you with such harshness, for from what I know of him, he is a fairly gentle soul."

"Perhaps his obvious interest in Lady Christina has made him act in a way contrary to his character." Lady

Frederica looked away from him and then back to Alice. "How are you, my dear? I am sorry that you have endured so much this evening already!"

Alice managed a small smile.

"I am quite all right, save for a sore arm. I did not once expect Lady Christina to express such a strength of feeling for Lord Sedgewick! She has not often been in his company and–"

"Mayhap she wishes to be," Lady Frederica interrupted, nudging Alice lightly. "She sees how interested Lord Sedgewick is in your company, and is now jealous of it."

A faint heat warmed Alice's cheeks as she looked back at her friends.

"You have noticed, then, that Lord Sedgewick is a little more in my company of late?"

"Noticed?" Miss Fairley laughed and nodded. "Of course we have noticed! I think it an excellent thing, though I do hope that something comes of it, and he does not simply linger in your company for a time before departing."

A flurry of excitement rushed through Alice, and she caught her breath, though she lowered her head and, clasped her hands, bringing them to her chin so that her friends would not see the strength of her reaction. Might it be that Lord Sedgewick would consider her to be a connection of special significance? That he might seek to court her? Could she, as a wallflower, let herself believe such a thing?

"I think that he is an excellent gentleman." Miss

Fairley smiled as Alice looked at her. "I can see that you are eager for more of his company, certainly."

"Of course I am!" Alice could not help but exclaim, making her friends laugh. "He is a kind, generous, amiable gentleman who seems eager for my company, and I will admit to being eager for his in return."

Both of her friends smiled, though Alice was sure that there was a hint of sadness hidden there also. Her heart ached for them and, at the same time, grew a little fearful for her own circumstances. What if Lord Sedgewick, despite his interest in her company, decided not to take their connection any further? If her heart was already seeking him out if there was an interest there that she could not deny, then would it not break if he decided to step away?

"Let us hope that all will turn out as you hope," Miss Fairley murmured, as if she had been able to read all of Alice's thoughts and now wished to comfort her. "And that Lady Christina causes no more difficulties for you!"

Alice managed a wry smile as Lady Frederica nodded her agreement with all that Miss Fairley had said.

"That is something I shall *certainly* wish for," she answered with a smile. "Though mayhap I ought to share it with Lord Sedgewick also? Mayhap he does not know of her interest, and it would be wise for me to tell him?"

"I think that he would appreciate knowing what has taken place, yes." Lady Frederica tilted her head. "But do not worry that in telling him of it, he will then turn to Lady Christina rather than look to you. Trust me, my dear friend, if he has taken no note of her already, then he will not do so simply because you tell him of her interest."

Taking a deep breath, Alice tried to believe what her friend said and, with a nod, silently promised to herself that she would speak to Lord Sedgewick about what had taken place at the very first opportunity. She could only hope that it would not break their strong connection apart entirely.

CHAPTER FOURTEEN

"So you felt nothing whatsoever?"

Simon grimaced.

"No, I certainly had an ache in my stomach, much as I had endured before, though it was not at all of the same intensity, for which I was grateful!"

"Then someone is still attempting to poison you." Lord Larbert frowned and shook his head. "It is a good deal more serious than I had at first anticipated, Sedgewick. This is not something that can be ignored. I would urge you to consider what it is you are to do."

"I can do nothing!" Simon threw up his hands and then sighed. "I can do nothing at all, for I have no knowledge of who is attempting to do this, or of their reasons behind it. I have made no enemies save for Lord Cartwright and, having already confronted him, I quickly learned that he has no blame in this whatsoever."

Lord Larbert's frown grew all the more severe.

"I do not know what to suggest, but something must be done. You cannot go through the Season in such a state as this - always afraid to eat or to drink anything which is offered to you for fear that it may hold a poison which will render you severely unwell."

"Or worse," Simon muttered, seeing his friend's eyebrows lift. "I do not know what this person's intentions are, Larbert. What if they intend something more sinister? What if I am destined for the grave? What if their only hope for me is to see me at death's door?"

The dark look on Lord Larbert's face lifted just a little.

"I do not think that someone seeks to kill you, my friend. If they had done – and I do not mean this to be callous – I believe that they would have done so long before now. To bring someone to the end of their life is a severe punishment indeed, and you have done nothing to warrant such destruction!"

"Then what is the reason for it?"

Lord Larbert let out a slow breath.

"I do not know," he answered, eventually. "Did this person wish to stop you from stepping out to dance?"

"With Lady Alice? I can hardly think that would be a reason."

"Unless," Lord Larbert continued, slowly, "it was not because of Lady Alice. Mayhap they wished you to stop dancing entirely – for the rest of the evening, in fact!"

"So I could not dance with anyone else?" Simon queried as his friend nodded. "I suppose... I suppose that might make sense. I–" A tap at the door interrupted him and, clearing his throat, he called for his staff to enter. It was the butler who, bowing, stepped aside thereafter.

"Lady Alice, my Lord, accompanied by Lady Frederica."

Simon rose to his feet immediately, as Lord Larbert did the same. The two young ladies came in at once, followed by their maids, and Simon smiled, bowing to them both, but his gaze fixed on Lady Alice thereafter. Last evening, he had been very glad indeed to have been well enough to dance with her, though his stomach had been terribly painful at the same time. She had said something about wishing to speak with him, but he had not realized that she had meant to call on him.

But I am very glad that she has chosen to do so.

"How excellent to see you again, Lady Alice… and you also, Lady Frederica." Simon gestured to the chairs opposite him. "Please, do be seated." Telling the butler to bring them refreshments immediately, he returned his gaze to Lady Alice and took her in. She was smiling gently, but the way her eyes darted from left to right told him that there was something troubling her. He did not wait a second more to ask her what the reason for her visit was. "Tell me, what was it that you wished to speak with me about?"

Lady Alice's eyes flared in surprise, only to settle again when she clearly remembered telling him of her desire the previous evening.

"Last evening, I had an encounter with Lady Christina."

"A dreadful one!", Lady Frederica gestured to Lady Alice's arm and Simon immediately caught his breath, taking in the purple and blue bruises which ran down her arm towards her hand. "She grasped Lady Alice so very tightly that Alice could not get free!"

As Simon tried to find something to say, his shock stealing his words away, Lady Alice set her hand on top of Lady Frederica's and smiled.

"I am quite all right. It is only a bruise." Settling her hands in her lap, she took a breath and then continued. "Lady Christina was most displeased with me – as you might be able to see!" Her smile grew rueful. "She made some demands upon me and when I refused, her grip grew all the tighter, and her anger rose all the more."

"And what demands were these?" Simon asked, his throat still tight, such was the shock of what he had seen. "Why should she do such a thing to you?"

Lady Alice licked her lips and then looked away.

"She... she demanded that I stay away from you, Lord Sedgewick. She stated that your reputation was tarnished because of your ongoing interest in my company, and that I ought to be much more considerate of that, and a good deal less selfish. When I did not accept what she had said, when I made it clear that I would not do as she demanded, simply because she commanded it, her anger grew even fiercer. Much to my relief, Lady Frederica and Miss Fairley came to my aid."

"Good gracious." Rather than feeling any sort of joy or interest in Lady Christina, Simon's heart clamored with upset and anger over what she had done to Lady Alice. "I am terribly sorry to hear of what has taken place. I can assure you, I have shown the lady not even the smallest flicker of interest and yet now, to know that she has expectations and makes demands is... somewhat disconcerting."

The arrival of the tea tray put an end to their conversation for a short while, though Simon's thoughts continued to weave this way and that when it came to Lady Alice and Lady Christina's imposition upon her. They were so very different and, though Lady Christina might now have an interest in his company, Simon could not have been more disinclined towards her.

"Thereafter, Lord Steelforth came to speak with Lady Alice." Simon blinked, his eyes going again to Lady Alice who simply nodded as Lady Frederica continued. "It was a very strange conversation, for first he demanded to know what it was that Lady Alice had done to upset Lady Christina – although I did not think that there was a strong connection between them – and thereafter, he seemed very upset indeed when he was informed that she had come to speak to Lady Alice about you."

"Mayhap he was envious." Lord Larbert lifted an eyebrow in Simon's direction. "There seems to me to be no other possible reason for his upset."

A tight hand gripped Simon's heart, and he shook his head, looking away.

"It is not the first time that Lord Steelforth has shown himself in that way. He spoke to me very harshly some time ago, though I have assured him that I have no particular interest in Lady Christina."

Lady Alice coughed lightly and spoke, though her gaze was now fixed on her hands.

"Mayhap it is not that you have no particular interest

in her, but rather that she has an interest in your company, Lord Sedgewick."

The tightness around his heart grew all the more and he scowled, wishing that he could express all that he admired about Lady Alice, and how little he thought of every other lady of his acquaintance.

And then, the realization of what he felt struck him so hard that he fought to catch his breath. His eyes grew a little glazed as he stared at Lady Alice, aware that she was not looking back at him but being relieved about that, given the intensity within his own heart. If he truly thought that highly of her, if he was honest with himself about his feelings, then he realized now that there was an affection there for her – an affection so strong that he could not remove it from himself and, indeed, did not *want* to even attempt to do so. Never had he thought that he would find himself drawn to a wallflower and yet, as he had grown in his connection to her, Simon had begun to see that there was nothing aside from her company which he desired. He had come to care very little for all that the *ton* might think of him, had given barely a moment's consideration to how poorly they might view him, given his closeness to her. Lady Alice was all that he desired.

"Lord Sedgewick?"

Simon blinked rapidly, realizing now that Lady Alice had lifted her head and was gazing back at him, though he had not noticed it until this moment.

"My apologies." Reaching for his tea, he took a draught and let the few moments of silence pass. "You may well be right as regards Lady Christina and Lord

Steelforth, but that does not concern me. If Lord Steelforth wishes to pursue Lady Christina, then I wish him the very best of luck."

A smile tipped Lady Alice's lips.

"I do not think that Lady Christina would be particularly happy to hear you say such a thing."

"But I do not care about Lady Christina, not in any way," he replied, quickly. "I am terribly sorry that she did such a thing to you. That is unconscionable and, if you wish, I shall speak to her about her behavior."

Quickly, Lady Alice shook her head.

"Thank you, but that will not be necessary. I am only glad that you are not severely unwell, as you were before."

"Thanks to your hasty action." Simon, seeing the questioning look on Lord Larbert's face, quickly explained. "Lady Alice practically knocked the glass from my hand, though I had already taken a sip. Had she not reminded me, had she not *prevented* me, then I would have drunk the entire measure and then, no doubt, would have been gravely ill again."

"And unable to dance."

Simon nodded, wondering at the way that Lady Alice had spoken those words. They had been slow and dragged out as though she were thinking quickly yet speaking so slowly so as to allow her thoughts to settle within her mind at the same time. Her eyes were darting here and there, and she snatched in a breath sharply, lifting her head to look straight into his eyes.

"That is why you were given the brandy!" she

exclaimed, her eyes flaring wide. "So that you could not dance."

A frown pulled at Simon's brow.

"Yes, I thought that we had accepted that."

"But it was not a deliberate act against *me*," Lady Alice continued, sounding all the more excited as she leaned forward in her chair. "It was simply… accidental. That is to say, it was only by chance that you took those two drinks at the times that you took them. I have no doubt that the footman was told to bring the brandy to you, and that he might very well have missed being able to do so on one or two occasions prior to the one on which you actually took the glass. Mayhap you did not take it when it was offered to you first, mayhap you did not notice it, or had another drink in your hand already. Regardless, when you *did* take it, it came at the same time as our waltz was to take place, though I think now that it was not a deliberate intent for it to injure you at that particular time. It was, instead, a desire to have you removed from the ballroom entirely, so that you might not get to dance with any other young lady."

The words Lady Alice spoke reached Simon, slipping into his mind, and making his eyes flare in understanding.

"You mean to suggest, then, that a gentleman or a lady desired me to be unable to stand up with anyone?"

"A gentleman is most likely, is it not?" Lord Larbert's tone of voice was a little higher than before, his eyes rounding as he looked to Lady Alice. "You believe that it might be Lord Steelforth!"

Simon's gaze shot to Lady Alice, seeing her nod, and

as the realization hit him all at once, he collapsed back into his chair and stared blankly straight ahead.

It was all so very clear. If Lord Steelforth was as upset and as envious as Lady Alice had described, then might he not have done something to keep Simon away from Lady Christina?

"You have danced often with Lady Christina, have you not?" Lord Larbert asked, as Simon nodded slowly, running one finger over his lips as he thought hard. "Then Lord Steelforth might have found such dances to be more than he could bear and thereafter, decided to take matters into his own hands."

"By poisoning me." Simon let the words settle as he spoke them, hearing nothing now but his own breathing, which was coming quickly. "Do you truly think that he might do something like that?"

"There is no way to prove it." Lady Frederica tucked a stray curl behind her ear as she looked from one to the other. "You could determine to go to Lord Steelforth and demand to know the truth, but whether you would get it from him, I could not say."

"And I highly doubt it," Lord Larbert interrupted. "A gentleman is not about to admit to any such wrongdoing and, to my mind, would not even state that he has an interest in Lady Christina! What good would it do him? It might make him the talk of London and he would not want such a thing as that. It would damage his reputation if it were known that he had been pursuing a young lady to the point of injuring another gentleman who had shown a little interest in her."

A slight buzzing in Simon's ears had him leaning

forward and picking up his tea again so that he might have something to do. Part of him believed that they had found the right gentleman, that Lord Steelforth *was* the gentleman who had injured him, but there was still a good deal of doubt. If they could not prove it, then what was to prevent Lord Steelforth from trying to do such a thing again?

"You must be all the more cautious," Lord Larbert murmured, clearly a good deal concerned for Simon's wellbeing. "If Lord Steelforth realizes that you are not eating or drinking as you usually do, then he will understand that you have discovered the truth, and who can say what it is he will do then?"

"I do not think that he would do anything more severe than what he has already done," Simon said firmly, catching the look of concern that flared in Lady Alice's eyes. "But yes, if it is Lord Steelforth, doing what he can to make certain that I stay far from Lady Christina then I must be on my guard."

"And mayhap, if I might be so bold as to suggest such a thing, stay a little further away from Lady Christina." This time, when Lady Alice spoke, it was with a hint of warmth in her voice, as though she were close to teasing him. "I think that would solve a great many problems, and take away any sort of difficulty."

"You are quite right. I have every intention of doing as you suggest." The smile he returned to her held within it a measure of affection that he was certain he could not hide from her – or from anyone who saw his gaze towards her at that moment. "As I have said, I have no interest in Lady Christina, nor in Lady Helen, for that matter, though they both appear to be quite enamored of my company."

"I cannot think why," Lord Larbert added, dryly. "Though given that Lady Helen has managed to demand a masquerade ball from you, mayhap *that* is the reason that she enjoys your company so much. You are much too pliable."

A little embarrassed, Simon waved a hand in his friend's direction.

"You know very well that came about from my lack of concentration, which again speaks of my lack of desire for her company!" A flick of his eyes towards Lady Alice told him that she was laughing quietly, and he found himself joining in with her, relieved that she did not take anything Lord Larbert had said with any seriousness. "Though on this occasion, I am glad that it has come about, since I will be able to have you both present, Lady Frederica and Lady Alice, alongside all of your friends."

Lady Alice's eyes swirled with flashes of excitement.

"We are very much looking forward to it." Her smile slipped. "Though what of Lord Steelforth? What shall you do in that regard?"

Simon hesitated, then shrugged.

"I shall speak to him directly. I will not accuse him, but I will inform him that I have no interest in Lady Christina and that he is not to have any concern. Mayhap that will be enough to prevent him from continuing with such a vendetta against me!" Looking to Lord Larbert, he shrugged. "Mayhap I shall go this very afternoon."

"I would be glad to join you," his friend answered, evidently hearing the question in Simon's voice.

"Then we should take our leave so you might–"

"No, no, please do not hurry away!" Half out of his chair, Simon gestured for Lady Alice to remain where she was and when she sat back into her chair, he relaxed and let himself sit back also. "I would much rather linger in your company than go pursuing Lord Steelforth."

When her eyes met his, it was as if there were only the two of them in the room. The corners of her mouth edged upwards, and Simon's breath caught in his chest, leaving his heart pounding furiously, his mouth going dry as fire rose up in his chest. The connection between them was undeniable, his desire for more of her irrefutable. Had Lord Larbert and Lady Frederica been absent, then Simon was quite certain that he would have gone to her at once, taken her hands in his, and confessed all that he felt – in the hope that she would return his affection.

"More tea, then?" It was Lord Larbert's interruption that had Simon pulling his gaze away from Lady Alice, aware of the heated emotions running wildly through him. "And perhaps a cake or two?"

"Of course," Simon muttered, though try as he might, he could not stop the warm, broad smile from spreading across his face and remaining there. Simon was beginning to believe that it would never truly fade, for as long as he was in the presence of Lady Alice, for as often as he so much as *thought* of her, that smile returned to him with an ever increasing strength.

It was more wonderful than he had ever imagined.

CHAPTER FIFTEEN

Alice placed the mask on her face, took a deep breath, and set her shoulders before walking towards the ballroom. The moment that she stepped inside, a hand reached out to catch hers and Alice laughed softly, seeing the very mask which Miss Simmons had shown her the previous day.

"Good evening, Miss Simmons."

"Is this not wonderful?"

Smiling, Alice nodded.

"It is." Looking around the ballroom, Alice took in all of the wonderful sights, her heart leaping with excitement. "And here we all are, just as any other guest might be."

"Indeed." Miss Simmons let out a slow breath and then smiled. "It is more than I ever anticipated or expected – and it holds so much beauty within it, I can hardly believe that I am permitted to be a part of it."

"It is just as you deserve," a voice murmured, one that

Alice recognized as Miss Bosworth's. "Recall, we are just as any other guests here. We have as much right to stand amongst them as anyone else. We must not let ourselves fall back to the shadows or be overwhelmed by all that is offered to us."

Lady Frederica slipped her arm through Alice's, her own mask simple but yet still hiding her features, though Alice recognized her immediately.

"Quite right, Miss Bosworth. And who knows? We may find ourselves caught by an exceptional gentleman this evening, who will have no choice but to marry us, since he will fall quite in love with us almost at once."

Alice laughed, though her thoughts then returned to Lord Sedgewick, remembering how warmly he had looked at her the last time they had spoken together. There had been something more in his gaze then, something more that she had seen, but been too uncertain, too unsure, of what it might be to allow herself to hope. How much she wished that it was an affection for her, given that her own heart was already filled with an affection for him!

"Do you wish to go and find him?"

Alice looked up at Lady Frederica, seeing her friend's grin and laughing with a mixture of both embarrassment at being so obvious and yet anticipation at being in Lord Sedgewick's company again.

"I do."

"Then let us step out together. Your mother will not mind?"

Shaking her head no, Alice excused herself from the

rest of her friends and walked along the edge of the ballroom with Lady Frederica – not because she wished to cling to the shadows, but because she wanted very much to spy Lord Sedgewick and, though it would be difficult enough given that everyone was wearing a mask, this would be the best place for her to seek him out.

"Did he tell you what mask he would be wearing?"

"He did." Alice smiled at her friend. "I received a note earlier today informing me that, while he had every intention of speaking to Lord Steelforth before the Masquerade, he had not yet found the opportunity. I believe that, when they went to call, Lord Steelforth was not at home and thus, given how much Lord Sedgewick had to do by way of preparation, he did not have any further opportunity."

"So will he speak to him this evening?"

Alice nodded.

"Yes, he said that he would do so, just as soon as he was able. He also informed me that his mask would be black, with a single raven feather at one side. Very simple, but at the same time, very distinctive."

Lady Frederica nodded, her head turning to look over her shoulder.

"I do hope that, once this business with Lord Steelforth is finished, you might then begin to think of your own connection to Lord Sedgewick."

A tightness came into Alice's throat, and she swallowed hard, glancing up at her friend.

"Do you think that he might feel something akin to what is in my own heart?"

Lady Frederica laughed, her eyes twinkling behind her mask.

"Of course I do! I am sure that I have said so to you before, but I saw it all the more clearly when we went to call on him together. My dear friend, that gentleman is quite lost in an affection for you, and I shall be glad indeed when it is not only identified, but brought to you, alongside the fierce and furious hope that you will be willing to step into place beside him."

Aware now that Lady Frederica spoke of matrimony, Alice shook her head, her heart fluttering.

"I do not think that I can let myself hope for something as profound as that. Not as yet, at least."

"I think – oh! Look, is that not he?"

Taking in the gentleman Lady Frederica had pointed out, Alice's heart flung itself hard at her ribs as he turned, his gaze catching hers. Yes, this was Lord Sedgewick, she was sure of it. Even without the identifiable mask, she would be certain to have recognized him anywhere. Without so much as a word, she made her way towards him but then stayed a step or two back, hearing him speak to another gentleman.

"I can assure you that I am being entirely truthful," Lord Sedgewick stated, quite clearly. "I have told you that I have no interest in furthering my connection with Lady Christina, and I beg of you to believe it." Realizing now that he was speaking to Lord Steelforth, Alice shared a glance with Lady Frederica, only for Lord Sedgewick to turn to them both, one arm spreading out towards her. "As I was saying, Steelforth, I have no interest in Lady Christina's company over any other. I have my own considerations and they do not include her."

Catching the glance that Lord Steelforth sent in her direction, Alice went to lower her eyes, only to remember that she was wearing a mask. Looking back at Lord Steelforth with a steadiness she did not truly feel, Alice moved closer to Lord Sedgewick and smiled when he put his arm out so that she might settle her hand upon it.

"I see." Lord Steelforth ran one hand over his chin, the top half of his features hidden by a large, gold mask that spread out like a crown over his forehead. "And you say this is the truth, Lord Sedgewick?"

"It is." The strength of his voice left an impression even upon Alice and as she looked back at Lord Steelforth, she saw him nod slowly. "I would not have come to speak to you otherwise, would I?"

"And you know that Lord Sedgewick is a man of his word," Alice put in, wanting now to support Lord Sedgewick, so that he could be spared from any more pain or illness. "He is not a gentleman known for his lies, for his misdeeds or his deliberate falsehoods, is he?"

A small smile tugged at Lord Steelforth's lips.

"That is true enough, my Lady," he agreed, inclining his head. "And you seem very eager to come to his defense."

Fire burst in Alice's cheeks, but she kept her gaze firm.

"I do not want anyone to think poorly of Lord Sedgewick. I do not think that there is anything wrong with that."

Lord Steelforth grinned and nodded again, though this time, his gaze went to Lord Sedgewick himself.

"I suppose that is true. It seems that you have found a defense for yourself, Lord Sedgewick… and therefore, I will admit that I am inclined to believe you."

A breath of relief escaped from Lord Sedgewick's lips, though it was only loud enough for Alice herself to hear.

"I am glad to hear it. Let us part as friends, Lord Steelforth. I wish you good fortune when it comes to seeking out a lady of your choosing."

Lord Steelforth laughed but the sound was harsh and ragged, making Alice wince.

"Would that I had some luck, Lord Sedgewick," he retorted, and a hint of anger jagged through his words. "Mayhap once the lady realizes that you are not considering her, she might permit *me* to call upon her instead."

"I am sure that she will."

Putting on as bright a smile as she could, Alice's breath coiled in her chest as Lord Steelforth looked first to her and then back to Lord Sedgewick again before, finally, nodding and turning away with only a mumbled, 'good evening' by way of parting.

"That must have been a delicate conversation." Alice smiled when Lord Sedgewick blew out a long breath, seeing him nod. "I am sure that you did very well."

"I am only glad that he now understands that I have no interest in Lady Christiana." Inclining his head, Lord Sedgewick smiled at her. "Might you dance this evening, my Lady?"

Alice took the dance card from her wrist and held it out to him.

"But of course, my Lord," she replied, recalling that they were not meant to know one another at this present moment. "I thank you."

"Capital. And might I have your dance card also, my Lady?" Having requested both the dance card of Alice and that of Lady Frederica, Lord Sedgewick wrote down his initials on their dance cards and then returned them. "I look forward to being able to step out with each of you."

Looking down at her dance card, Alice caught her breath as she saw where Lord Sedgewick had placed his name. Not only had he taken her waltz, but he had also taken another of the dances, meaning that she would be stepping out twice with him. That would surely draw the attention of the *ton*, would it not?

I am wearing a mask. No one will know who I am. Her heart dropped suddenly as a small frown pulled at her forehead. *Is that why Lord Sedgewick is dancing twice with me now? Because my identity is hidden from them all?*

"I should hope that you will stay until the unmasking."

Alice's head shot up quickly.

"I beg your pardon, Lord Sedgewick?"

A smile began to lift her heart back to the dizzying heights it had been at only a few moments ago.

"I wondered if you had any intention of remaining at the ball until the unmasking. I should very much like it if you would linger until then. I should like the *ton* to see that you are someone of importance to me."

It was as though he had seen the fears that had clouded her mind and had wanted, thereafter, to put them all to rest. Alice clasped both hands together and smiled, though her throat constricted with the strength of emotion that roared through her. Lord Sedgewick *wanted* her face to be shown to all and sundry, wanted her to be standing by him so that the *ton* could see just how close they had become. Could there be any more evidence of his affection for her than that?

"I shall have to speak to my mother but yes, I am certain that I will be able to do so. I–"

"You *must* be Lord Sedgewick." A young lady stepped directly in between Alice and Lord Sedgewick, one fan fluttering gently in her hand. "I recognize your voice."

Alice frowned, looking at Lady Frederica who only shrugged lightly. As the lady continued to speak, Alice's gaze went to a gentleman standing a little further back. He did not come closer, did not make to join the conversation, but rather stood where he was, his hands clasped behind his back and his gaze, from what she could see, fixed directly on the lady in front of her.

"I will not confirm that to be true, I am afraid," Lord Sedgewick replied, his expression rather resolute. "I do hope that you are enjoying the evening."

"And will you not ask me to dance?"

Again, Alice shared a glance with Lady Frederica, rather surprised that a young lady should be so forward. Then again, she considered, this was a Masquerade, so it did not particularly matter what the *ton* might think of such behavior, given that they would not know who was behind it.

"But of course." There was a roughness to Lord Sedgewick's voice which had been absent before and Alice dropped her gaze as he took the dance card from the young lady to write his name there. Uncertain as to whether or not she ought to move away, she was rather surprised when another gentleman bowed his head to her, taking her attention away from Lord Sedgewick.

"You are one of the most beautiful young ladies at the ball, I am certain of it," the gentleman told her, just as another came into view, stepping close to the first. "I must sign your dance card!"

"As must I!" declared the second, leaving Alice with very little else to do other than hand her dance card over to them both.

She made to say something to Lady Frederica, only for Lady Frederica's attention to be caught by an entirely different gentleman who, again, asked for her dance card. Alice began to smile, seeing the joy sparking through Lady Frederica's eyes and realizing now that this was what every young lady of the *ton* experienced. This was what she had been missing, what she had forgotten about – and yet, though there was happiness in having her dance card filled, there was also an awareness that this was not what brought her the greatest joy. Instead, it was the anticipation of stepping out with Lord Sedgewick that made her smile, the excitement of once more being in his arms. The other dances and the other gentlemen would be pleasant enough, certainly, but the only person she wished to be in company with was Lord Sedgewick.

~

"The first of our two dances, my Lord."

Lord Sedgewick grinned.

"It is. I must admit, however, that it has been rather difficult to recall which young lady I am to dance with next, given that I have had to write a description of their mask and the color of their gown or their hair upon my dance card – though some I have recognized, I will admit."

"Oh?"

Alice curtsied as the music began and Lord Sedgewick bowed low.

"I have recognized your friends, of course, for the smiles upon their faces are, to my mind, bigger than any other. Some I have recognized from their voice and others from their... enthusiasm and boldness."

Alice turned away from him for a moment as her steps led her from one place to the next.

"Do you mean that Lady Christina–"

"Yes, *and* Lady Helen, though Lady Helen was the first, I am sure of it."

Remembering the gentleman who had been glowering at Lord Sedgewick as he had signed his name to a dance card, Alice frowned.

"Then which gentleman was it who..." Seeing his confusion, she stopped speaking and smiled. "It does not matter. All I am glad of is–"

A sudden, sharp inhale cut off her words as Lord Sedgewick stopped suddenly and dropped his head, one hand going to his stomach. The dancing continued around them and Lord Sedgewick, now going very pale indeed, attempted to continue – but Alice knew precisely what was happening.

"You are unwell again." With a scowl, she stepped closer, took his arm, and then began to lead him to the side of the ballroom, heedless of the other guests. After all, they were all still wearing masks, so who would be able to tell who she was and what she was doing? "Mayhap if you see the physician quickly, it may not be as severe."

Snapping his fingers, Lord Sedgewick sent one of his footmen scurrying off to find the physician, while Alice and another footman helped him to the door, stepping out into the hallway and thereafter, into the small parlor beyond.

"What has happened?" Alice turned her head just as Lord Larbert pulled the mask from his face and hurried into the room. "I saw you guiding Lord Sedgewick back into this room," he said, by way of explanation, his expression tight with concern. "You cannot be ill again, surely?"

"I am." Lord Sedgewick let out a groan, his eyes squeezing tight closed as one hand gripped at his stomach, his mask already discarded to the floor. "I thought – I thought speaking with Lord Steelforth would bring the situation to an end but..."

Alice took his other hand in hers, seeing the sweat breaking out across his forehead.

"It might not have been Lord Steelforth," she murmured, as Lord Sedgewick groaned again. "It might have been someone entirely different, someone we have not considered as yet."

"But who?" Lord Larbert demanded, striding around the room as though doing so would be of some use to someone. "Who would have done this to Lord Sedgewick and for what purpose?"

"I–"

Alice's thoughts were broken as the physician hurried into the room, stating that he had been close by when he had seen the footman leave the house and how glad he was of that. Quickly, he took a small vial from his bag and soon, a glass containing a mouthful of water and a few drops of this concoction was handed to Lord Sedgewick. His eyes went to hers, a pleading settling there, and Alice rose to her feet, letting go of his hand.

"I will take my leave. I do hope that you recover quickly, Lord Sedgewick."

"He will," the physician assured her, as she made her way to the door. "I was here more quickly than before and so the purging will happen a good deal more quickly."

"I – I will come to find you." Lord Sedgewick gripped at his stomach again, doubling over in clear agony. "Thank you, Lady Alice."

There was nothing more for her to do than step away, reluctant though she was to do it, and return to the ballroom. All the while, however, her mind began to run through what she had seen, the gentleman she had witnessed glaring at Lord Sedgewick and, as she stepped back into the ballroom, Alice's heart began to sink.

They had placed guilt upon the wrong person. Thinking that Lord Steelforth was to blame, they had never once considered that there might be *another* gentleman pursuing yet another lady who was showing an interest in Lord Sedgewick.

They had made a mistake and now Lord Sedgewick was the one suffering for it.

CHAPTER SIXTEEN

Wobbling, Simon remained steadfast as he rose from his chair, relieved that the pain had already left him.

"It seems as though your quick arrival has brought about a rapidity of relief to my symptoms which I have not experienced before – though my strength is still somewhat lacking."

The physician nodded as he packed up his bag.

"It is to be expected. You will regain it quickly also, of course."

"But not in time for the end of the ball," Lord Larbert murmured, as Simon grimaced. "Come now, you cannot think to return to the dance?"

"I think that I must. It must be shown to the perpetrator that I am well enough to stand and–"

"But certainly not well enough to dance," the physician interjected. "Do be careful, Lord Sedgewick. To push yourself now would be to injure yourself further."

Simon scowled all the darker and then sat back down in his chair, waving one hand at Lord Larbert.

"Go, then. I will tell the staff that you are the one to whom they should go, should there be any questions or concerns. I, I think, will have to retire to my bed. I am very weary."

This was said with a heaviness that clung to his soul and continually pulled it low, leaving his head to droop forward and his shoulders to round.

"Do that." Lord Larbert came across the room and put one hand to Simon's shoulder. "And do not feel any displeasure over it. Yes, we thought that we had found the person behind this poisoning, but we had not. A little more thought must be given to the matter now, yes, but we are not able to do so at the present moment. Instead, you must rest and recover, and tomorrow, when Lady Alice comes to call on you, as I am certain that she will do, we can discuss the matter then in its entirety. Mayhap she will have another idea."

"She said something," Simon murmured, looking up at his friend as Lord Larbert began to make his way to the door. "What was it she spoke of? She said something about it being someone we had not considered as yet."

Lord Larbert turned.

"Yes, but that is quite obvious now, is it not? It *must* be someone we have not considered, it must be someone else."

"But she spoke with a determination which made me believe that she knew precisely who she was considering, now that we believe it cannot be Lord Steelforth," Simon continued, though he leaned his head back as he spoke, weary now. "Who might it be?"

"That is a question for tomorrow," Lord Larbert said, firmly. "I shall return to the ball, and you must rest. I will call upon you tomorrow, at your earliest convenience."

"Please," Simon said, sitting up a little straighter as Lord Larbert made his way to the door. "Might you find Lady Alice for me? Might you tell her that I am truly sorry for what has taken place given that it was to be an exceptional evening and to ask her if she might call tomorrow? I would like to see her again very soon."

"Of course you would," Lord Larbert replied, a grin edging up one side of his mouth despite the circumstances. "Yes, I shall tell her. Now, go and rest so that this malady might be gone from you just as soon as it is able."

Simon nodded and put his head back, his eyes already closing. His body was weak and sore, but his thoughts were a little happier. Tomorrow, he would see Lady Alice again and, very soon, he wanted to speak to her of his heart, of the affection within it for her. As yet, he had not said a single word to her of such things but there was a desire to do so now. Seeing her smile as he had written his name on her dance card, seeing the light and the happiness in her eyes, had confirmed to him that yes, she was the only one he wanted to have in his arms.

And it was time to tell her.

∽

"I AM SO VERY glad to see you recovered."

Simon smiled and got to his feet, though Lady Alice

did not stop to curtsey. Instead, she rushed forward and grasped his hands in hers, looking up into his face, her eyes searching his.

"I am quite well, I assure you."

"I could hardly believe it when I saw you begin to wane," she said, her voice a little hoarse now. "It was dreadful though, of course, it must have been a good deal more difficult for you."

"It was more frustrating than anything else," he answered, with a chuckle. "I thought that I had set the matter to rest, that there was no reason for restraint with brandy and the like – especially at my own ball – but it seems that we were wrong in our considerations!"

"For which I am truly sorry."

Simon squeezed her hands lightly and shook his head.

"There is nothing for you to apologize for, Lady Alice. It was not your fault."

"Mayhap I should not have been so certain. I think... I think that while my idea was correct, it was the wrong gentleman who I identified."

Simon gestured to her to sit down only to realize that Lady Frederica was sitting there also. Flushing hot, he quickly cleared his throat and made to apologize, only for the door to sail open and Lord Larbert to stride in.

"Ah, I have not missed the start of the conversation, I hope?"

"No, not at all." Rather grateful for the interruption, Simon gestured to a vacant chair. "Lady Alice was about to explain to me what she meant by this 'wrong gentleman'."

He turned his attention back to Lady Alice who, her cheeks a little flushed, nodded.

"I was glad to see Lord Sedgewick so recovered," she began, looking to Lord Larbert, who smiled, "but when I was taking my leave of you both yesterday, I recalled something – nay, some*one*, I had seen last evening during the ball."

"Who?" Lord Larbert spoke before Simon could. "Who was he?"

"I – I do not know. I could not make out his face, because everyone was masked. But there was a young lady who pushed between me, and Lord Sedgewick, do you recall?" Swirling brown eyes turned towards him. "Do you recall?"

Simon nodded.

"I do. And I knew precisely who it was as well, given her voice and her manner." Seeing three pairs of eyes focused on him, he shrugged. "It was Lady Helen."

"Lady Helen," Lord Larbert repeated, though he did not sound as though he had reached any sort of understanding. "What gentleman pursues her? I cannot think of any."

Lady Alice spread out her hands.

"I do not know either, but I was certainly all too aware of a particular gentleman watching her as she spoke with you, Lord Sedgewick. He did not appear to be at all pleased and, in truth, I began to be a trifle concerned about what might occur should the conversation continue."

Closing his eyes, Simon took a deep breath and then released it again.

"I have an idea of who it might be."

"You do?"

Lady Alice's exclamation had his eyes flaring, only for him then to smile a little wryly.

"Yes, I believe that I do. I have had one encounter with a gentleman who was most displeased with my interest in the lady. In fact, he warned me to stay away from her."

"Which you have not done," Lord Larbert murmured, causing Lady Alice to shoot him a quick look. "That is not to say that you have any real interest in the lady, but you have been dancing and conversing with her."

"Which might make the gentleman in question all the more suspicious of your motivations," Lady Frederica added, quickly. "After all, he has asked you to stay back from Lady Helen and you have not done so. Therefore, he sees it as his right to... *encourage* you to do as he has asked."

Simon shook his head.

"I do not understand why he would do such a thing, when I have already made it plain that I have no interest in the lady! That seems nonsensical."

Lady Frederica tilted her head and smiled at him.

"You may have *said* such a thing, Lord Sedgewick, but Lord Westerly clearly did not believe you. After all, given that you continued to dance with her, and since she also sought you out for conversation, I can understand why he might find it less than believable that you had no interest in her company."

A dull ache settled in Simon's heart, and he let out an exasperated breath.

"But I danced with *many* a young lady. I have not, and did not, single her out!"

"And yet," Lady Alice interrupted, gently, "Lord Westerly's affection for Lady Helen, if that is what it is, has outweighed all of his good sense and driven him to do something drastic." Her shoulders lifted. "That is, if it *is* he who has been doing such things to you - although, if it was he I witnessed glaring at you last evening, I would be very surprised if it was not."

Simon took a deep breath, a slight shiver running down his spine.

"Goodness. That is a surprise."

"I might very well be wrong," Lady Alice began, but both Lord Larbert and Lady Frederica immediately shook their heads as Simon looked back at her.

"No, I think that you are quite right. I cannot quite believe that I did not think of this before now and, indeed, I am a little frustrated with myself for my lack of remembering about the conversations I have had with him!"

Silence ran around the room as Lady Alice exchanged a quick glance with Lady Frederica, but Simon was so deep in thought that he barely noticed the quiet. Why had he not realized this before? Why had he not thought that Lord Westerly might have something against him? After all, their first conversation about Lady Helen had been a little harsh and abrupt, but he had simply put it to the back of his mind and had forgotten about it.

That had been his error.

"What can be done now?"

Simon lifted his head and looked at his friend.

"I do not know, Larbert. What should I do? Confront him?"

"And what if he denies it?"

Pulling his mouth to one side, Simon hesitated as Lady Frederica's question rang around the room.

"Perhaps I hope that what I might say to him, what I will confront him about, will be sufficient for him to stop his vendetta against me?" Looking from one person to the other, he saw the doubt flickering in their expressions, and felt his own heart twinge with concern. "I do not know what else can be done."

Lady Alice straightened.

"You must catch him doing the very thing you suspect him of! He cannot deny it if he has been seen doing it."

"I agree," Simon answered, "but how is such a thing to be done? I cannot watch his every move, I cannot stand by his side in the hope of seeing him placing something in a glass of brandy and then directing a footman to me."

Lord Larbert chuckled, drawing Simon's attention.

"No, but *I* can."

"As can Lady Alice and I," Lady Frederica added as Lady Alice herself began to nod. "All you will have to do is seek out Lady Helen, make certain that her name is on your dance card, and thereafter, pray that one of us sees Lord Westerly doing as we suspect he will."

"And I could ask my friends to join us," Lady Alice suggested, as Lady Frederica let out a quiet exclamation of agreement. "Wallflowers are, it seems, good for hiding in the shadows but seeing a great deal. I am certain that together, we will be able to observe Lord Westerly. That way, you will have your proof and he will not be able to deny it."

Lord Larbert cleared his throat.

"There is one thing which you must *not* do, however," he began, speaking a little more slowly now, as his eyebrows dropped low. "You must not hold back as you have been doing. You must eat and drink just as any other person of society might do. Otherwise, Lord Westerly might be entirely unable to do as he wishes!"

"There is a little risk there, then." With a wry smile, Simon shrugged his shoulders. "I have been unwell on many an occasion now. Even if I should imbibe the poison for what will be yet another time, at least I will be assured that it will be the *last* time."

Lady Alice sat forward in her chair, her eyes large.

"We will do our utmost to make certain that such a thing does not take place." Glancing around, she reached out one hand to him as though she wanted to grasp his fingers in hers, only to drop her hand back to her lap again. "I do not want to see you unwell again, Lord Sedgewick, but Lord Larbert is correct. You must not hold yourself back."

Simon took a deep breath but nodded.

"I can do that," he promised, sensing the weight of their plan settling down upon his shoulders. "And once I hear from one of you that you have seen Lord Westerly do what we believe he will do, then I will go to him directly, confront him, and bring this whole matter to a close. Thereafter," he finished, never looking away from Lady Alice, "there is something more that I wish to say – something a good deal more significant, in fact, though it is to you I wish to speak, Lady Alice."

She smiled, her eyes holding a softness that had not been there before.

"I shall be glad to speak with you whenever the time is right," she said, quietly. "Thank you, Lord Sedgewick. Let us hope that this plan succeeds!"

CHAPTER SEVENTEEN

How much I wish I could go to him.
Watching Lord Sedgewick from where she stood at the back of the ballroom, Alice felt her heart reach out for him and yet she stayed where she was.

"It is not Lord Sedgewick we are meant to be watching." Lady Frederica giggled and nudged her, and Alice blushed furiously, her hands going to her cheeks. "Come now, take your eyes from him for just a little moment, if you can, and look instead to Lord Westerly. Look, *there* he is."

Alice looked in the direction Lady Frederica indicated and then let her gaze settle upon Lord Westerly. He was standing with his hands behind his back and ambling slowly around the room, looking all around with sharp eyes.

"Yes, that is the man who watched Lord Sedgewick," Alice murmured, as Lady Frederica dropped her hand. "His stance and his build are the same."

Lady Frederica turned her head and said the same to

Miss Fairley, who then spoke to the other wallflowers present. Alice watched as the young ladies moved away from one another, spreading out across the ballroom so that someone might always be watching Lord Westerly wherever he might go. Others would continue to steady their gaze on Lord Sedgewick. Aware of the tension beginning to wind through her, Alice watched carefully as Lord Westerly continued to walk towards them – only to then glance to where Lord Sedgewick stood, seeing him smiling and laughing with another young lady. Her heart immediately squeezed with both jealousy and a hint of pain but, reminding herself that this was precisely what he was *meant* to be doing, Alice took a long breath and continued to watch them both.

"Is that Lady Helen?"

Alice nodded.

"Yes, I think so."

"Look how Lord Westerly watches them." Lady Frederica shook her head. "There is an intensity in his gaze which speaks of anger – at least, it does to my mind. That is not a good thing, and certainly speaks in agreement to your suggestion that he is the one responsible for all that Lord Sedgewick has been plagued with."

"Indeed."

Pressing her hands together, Alice let her fingers link, squeezing them tight together. This was just as they had expected, but glaring at someone was not something she could hold against Lord Westerly. He had to *do* something, something which she could observe and, thereafter, report back to Lord Sedgewick.

"Look, he is moving away."

"Oh." Alice's shoulders dropped as she watched Lord Westerly turn around sharply and walk in the opposite direction from where Lady Helen and Lord Sedgewick stood. "That is not what I expected."

"Shall we walk together?" Lady Frederica suggested as Alice slipped her hand through her friend's arm. "We are wallflowers, are we not? I doubt Lord Westerly will even notice us even if we draw very close to him!"

A tightness came into Alice's throat as they stepped out together, finding comfort in the fact that the other wallflowers were watching both Lord Sedgewick and Lord Westerly. He would be able to do nothing without someone observing him, though the urgency to hurry after Lord Westerly tore through her and she quickened her steps.

"There."

Alice's heart began to thunder as she slowed her steps just enough to observe Lord Westerly stepping away from the other guests, making his way to the shadowed sides of the ballroom.

"Let us follow him. I – oh!"

Lady Frederica stopped at the same time as Alice did, seeing Lord Westerly taking a glass of brandy from the tray a footman held. Other guests moved in front of them, obscuring them from his view while, at the same time, permitting them to watch what he did.

"He – he is not drinking it." Alice gripped her friend's arm, seeing Lord Westerly move away and immediately going to follow him. "Where is he going now?"

Without a word, Lady Frederica stepped after Lord Westerly again. Alice released her friend's arm, forced to push her way through the ever-increasing number of guests whilst still attempting to keep her gaze fixed upon Lord Westerly.

And then, she saw it.

Standing by a pillar, she observed Lord Westerly as he pulled something from his pocket. Setting the glass of brandy down to the floor itself, he twisted the top of the vial, bent down, and tipped a few drops into it.

Alice's heart slammed hard against her ribs, and she caught her breath, turning to look at Lady Frederica with wide eyes.

"We have seen him do it!" she whispered, though Lady Frederica did not say a single word, her gaze still upon Lord Westerly. "I – oh, no!"

Her eyes rounded as she saw Lord Westerly hesitate and then, after a moment, tip in the rest of the vial until there was nothing left. Given that she did not know what was contained within it, her fear grew to such proportions, she could barely breathe. Lord Westerly had clearly put in a good deal more than he had first thought – which meant that, should Lord Sedgewick take the brandy, it would make him a good deal more unwell than before. What would such a heavy dose do to him? Panic gripped at her heart. "We must warn Lord Sedgewick."

Lady Frederica nodded.

"You go to him," she said, softly. "I will watch to see how he has that particular glass of brandy sent to Lord Sedgewick. That way, we will know every part of his plan and he will have no way to escape from it."

There was no time for her even to think of arguing. Instead, Alice turned on her heel and hurried back through the crowd, making her way back to where she had seen Lord Sedgewick.

But he was no longer there.

Her heart was like a bird frantically beating its wings, her skin prickling as she looked this way and that, trying to spy him. What if she could not find him in time? After all, Lord Larbert had told him that he had to be as any other guests, he had to eat and drink just as everyone else would – and that meant that, should the brandy come to him, as she suspected it would very soon, then he would drink it and yet again, become violently ill. What if the sheer amount Lord Westerly had put into the brandy was more than Lord Sedgewick's body could endure?

"He is dancing."

A quiet voice had Alice spinning around, her hands going to grip Miss Fairley's, her eyes wide.

"What did you say?"

"Lord Sedgewick is dancing with Lady Helen," Miss Fairley replied, looking at Alice with clear concern. "Why? What did you see Lord Westerly do?"

"Just as we thought – though he has tipped the vial entirely into the brandy! It seems to me that he has put an even greater dose into the brandy than before, and I *must* stop Lord Sedgewick from taking it." Her hands tightened on Miss Fairley's. "Is the dance almost at an end?"

"It is. Come, we will go to him together. Do not worry, you will reach him in time."

Alice's heart did not stop its frantic beating as she searched for Lord Sedgewick in the crowd of dancers, seeing them whirl and spin. Once the music began to slow, she brought her clasped hands to her mouth, her anxiety almost more than she could bear.

And then, his eyes found hers.

He smiled and she closed her eyes in relief, knowing now that he was safe, that he would be protected from whatever the poison Lord Westerly had placed in the brandy glass. Opening her eyes again, she looked back at him steadily, watching as he came closer to her, albeit with Lady Helen on his arm. When he turned and bowed, Lady Helen stepped back and curtsied, as was expected, before making her way back to her mother.

Lord Sedgewick began to walk toward Alice and Miss Fairley, only for a footman to move in between them, pausing for a moment to offer Lord Sedgewick the brandy that sat on the tray. With mounting horror, Alice watched Lord Sedgewick take it and, without hesitation, she rushed forward to grasp at his arm, practically knocking the footman back as she did so. The brandy sloshed from one side of the glass to the other though, thankfully, Lord Sedgewick had not brought any of it to his lips.

"I am all right," he murmured, as she let out a strangled exclamation. "I take it that Lord Westerly has done as you expected?"

Alice nodded, not able to speak, her breathing ragged.

"I believe that Lord Westerly has put in a little more than he first thought to." Miss Fairley came to stand by them, just as Lady Frederica appeared. "Lady Alice was deeply concerned for you."

"And I have witnessed Lord Westerly directing the brandy to go specifically to you."

Alice looked at Lady Frederica, whose smile was rather grim.

"The footman was given an extra coin or two for the trouble. I believe that we have more than enough to speak to Lord Westerly about."

"Why should you wish to speak to Lord Westerly?"

The unexpected appearance of Lady Helen had Alice blinking rapidly, though she did not much like the look of superiority that clung to Lady Helen's expression.

"Lord Sedgewick, pray come and speak with me for a short while," she continued, clearly not in the least bit interested in why they all wanted to converse with Lord Westerly. "I am without friend or company at the present and these wallflowers–"

"These wallflowers are exactly who *I* wish to speak with," Lord Sedgewick interrupted, making Lady Helen's eyes flare with surprise. "Lady Helen, while you might be unwilling to speak with these wonderful ladies, I have found myself delighted in their company – and by one in particular."

His gaze went to Alice who immediately blushed but found herself smiling at his kind compliment. Lady Helen, however, only narrowed her eyes.

"There is no reason for them to be speaking of Lord Westerly, however." Lady Helen lifted her chin, her eyes flashing. "I do not think *that* is necessary."

"It *is* necessary."

Alice spoke up, hearing her voice rasping with the stress of the situation.

"And why should that be?"

Turning, Alice looked up into the face of none other

than Lord Westerly, seeing his heavy frown and finding her stomach twisting with sudden anxiety. Were they to confront him now? Right here, at this present moment, in the middle of the ballroom?

"Mayhap you might wish to speak of this in a quieter place," Lord Sedgewick replied, though his voice and his gaze remained firm and steady.

"Speak of what?"

Lord Sedgewick lifted his chin.

"Should you like to take this brandy from me, Lord Westerly?" The challenge roared through his words and Alice caught the way that Lord Westerly flinched. "I have not touched it as yet. There can be nothing wrong with you taking it from me instead."

Alice's heart began to thud furiously as Lord Westerly's eyes narrowed, his jaw tightening as the other wallflowers and Lady Helen simply looked on, with the latter being clearly confused.

"I am sure that Lord Westerly can obtain his own brandy, Lord Sedgewick?" Lady Helen looked from Lord Sedgewick to Lord Westerly and then threw a look to Alice herself. "Whatever is the meaning of all of this?"

Lord Sedgewick cleared his throat.

"Mayhap you should like to tell Lady Helen the truth, Lord Westerly? Perhaps you will tell her that your envy, your jealousy has driven you to such lengths that you have decided to injure me in a manner which is both deceptive and cruel."

Lady Helen caught her breath, her eyes flaring wide.

"Lord Westerly? Surely this cannot be true!"

Alice looked at Lord Westerly and, as she had

expected, the gentleman shook his head. Lord Larbert stepped into the circle, his eyes a little narrowed as Lord Westerly continued on with his denial.

"Of course it is untrue! I have done nothing whatsoever. Lord Sedgewick is speaking utter nonsense."

"Then if that is so," Lord Sedgewick replied, just as quickly, "take this brandy and drink it before us all."

Lord Westerly snorted.

"I can obtain my own brandy if I wish. I do not need to touch yours."

"And would that be because of the vial of liquid which I witnessed you placing into Lord Sedgewick's brandy?" Unable to hold herself back, Alice stepped forward, her head lifting so she might gaze directly into Lord Westerly's face. "Both myself and Lady Frederica saw you doing so."

"As did I." Lord Larbert folded his arms across his chest. "You have been seen, Lord Westerly, by three sets of eyes."

Alice swallowed hard but then continued.

"And it is not the first time you have done such a thing either. On three previous occasions at least, you have poisoned Lord Sedgewick. He became so very ill that he could not stay on the dance floor, and was forced to retire early from the ball which he was attending. Thankfully, the third time, we were aware of what was taking place, and he only took a very small amount of the brandy. That must have been deeply frustrating for you - is that why you placed so much of that vial into his brandy this time?"

"Before you protest that we cannot state for certain

that the brandy which Lord Sedgewick holds is the very same as the one *you* held, let me make it quite clear that I followed that particular glass and saw the footman take it directly to Lord Sedgewick." With a small, wry smile, Lady Frederica tilted her head. "So you see, we are all very well aware of what it is that you have done."

Nothing but silence came from Lord Westerly. He stood and looked around the room, his eyes still narrowed but his mouth in a flat line. It was as if he had every intention of defending himself, but could not find the right words to express such a defense, given that there was evidence against him. Alice kept her stance steady, looking at Lord Westerly with a fixed gaze, ready to speak again about what she had witnessed, should it be required.

"Is this true, Lord Westerly?" Lady Helen's voice wobbled and, when Alice looked at her, there was a whiteness to her face which had not been there before. "Did you attempt to poison Lord Sedgewick so that he would not be able to dance with me – or to dance with anyone?" Lord Westerly shook his head, opened his mouth, and then snapped it shut again, running one hand through his hair before turning his head away. "Lord Westerly?" Lady Helen spoke again, though her voice was roughened this time as tears glistened in her eyes. "Pray be bold enough to tell the truth."

"What is it that you wish me to say?" Rather than speaking to Lord Sedgewick, or to any of the wallflowers, Lord Westerly turned his attention solely to Lady Helen. "I spoke to Lord Sedgewick. I warned him that I was to seek you out and to offer you my attentions and he *promised* me that he had no real interest in furthering his connection to you." A harsh laugh tore from his throat. "He said that, and I foolishly believed him, only to see him continuing with his attentions to you. He conversed with you, sought you out so that he might dance with you – what else was there for me to do? He is a Marquess, and I am not. Of *course* a young lady such as yourself would go to a gentleman with a higher title and thus, I thought..." Lord Westerly dropped his head and let out a low groan. "I thought that if I removed him from your sphere, then you might think to consider me instead."

Lady Helen gasped, one hand flying to her mouth as she stared, wide-eyed, at Lord Westerly. Alice blinked, then turned to Lord Sedgewick who was shaking his head.

"You admit to it, then. Well, I suppose that is the first honest thing you have done in some time." With a snort, Lord Sedgewick took a step closer to Lord Westerly, whose expression then changed from anger to fear. "I could call you out for this, Westerly. I could demand recompense. I could tell all of society what it is that you have done – and attempted to do – to me. What would have happened to me had I drunk this brandy? Do you have any knowledge of what would have taken place?"

Lord Westerly looked away, his face turning a little pale.

"I – I assume that you would have simply become ill as you did before. I put in a few drops into previous glasses, I did not think that a little more would be too different."

"That illness was so severe, it stole Lord Sedgewick's

strength!" Alice exclaimed before she could stop herself. "You had only put in a few drops previously – but now to put in the whole vial might have caused Lord Sedgewick to come close to death! You are foolishness itself, Lord Westerly, for doing such a thing so hastily, and without real thought. Your envy has driven you to recklessness. You cannot know how terrified I was, how scared I became in my attempts to reach Lord Sedgewick before the brandy came to his hand."

"You could have killed him!"

With a sob, Lady Helen turned and began to hurry away to the side of the ballroom and, without even a word of apology, Lord Westerly followed her. Alice stared, then shook her head, letting out a slow breath of relief as Lord Sedgewick's hand found hers.

"What will you do, Lord Sedgewick?" Miss Fairley offered him a small smile. "Shall you call him out? Seek recompense?"

Lord Sedgewick shook his head.

"I do not think so. What he did was grievous and foolish, but I shall not demand his life from him. However, I think a word or two in a few listening ears might be a wise idea. It would be good for other gentlemen to be aware of Lord Westerly's jealousy so that they might protect themselves, should it happen to them!"

"Mayhap Lady Helen will forgive him." Lady Frederica shrugged her shoulders when every eye turned to her. "It may sound a little odd, but mayhap Lady Helen will end up thinking well of Lord Westerly for his severe attempts to encourage her attentions."

"I must hope not!" Alice remarked as the other wallflowers laughed, clearly relieved that it had all now come to an end. "I cannot imagine such a thing!"

"Nor can I." Lord Sedgewick smiled and then released her hand, only to offer his arm. "Might we walk for a few minutes?"

Alice nodded, catching Lady Frederica's knowing smile and finding her own heart leaping furiously in her chest. With a glance and a nod of thanks to her friends and Lord Larbert, she stepped away with Lord Sedgewick, though they made their way to the back of the ballroom so that the shadows might hide them a little more. After all, even though she was a wallflower, she still ought to have a chaperone whilst walking with a gentleman.

"I feel a great weight lifted from my shoulders."

Lord Sedgewick let out a small sigh and Alice smiled up at him.

"As do I. I am so very glad that you are safe, and that no such illness will strike you again."

"As am I." Lord Sedgewick stopped their walk and turned to face her, her hand slipping from his arm. "However, now that I am free of this, now that there is no other distraction to be held before me, there is something more for me to confess."

Her heart began to quicken, but Alice did not so much as flinch. Instead, she merely nodded, looking at Lord Sedgewick, and waiting for him to continue.

"I am certain that you will already suspect this, but I confess to you now that my heart is already quite caught up with you, Lady Alice." Lord Sedgewick spoke with an openness and a frankness which Alice herself deeply appreciated, seeing him shrug and then smile. "My heart holds a growing affection for you, Lady Alice, and indeed I believe that I am already falling in love with you. I did not ever think that such emotions were possible for a gentleman such as I – indeed, I thought only to find a suitable lady – and yet, my heart has led me down an entirely different path." His jaw tightened for a moment, and he looked away. "I believe that, if you were to step away from me, if our connection was to be severed, then my heart would be quite broken. It would cause me more pain and agony than I have ever experienced before. I would ask you, Lady Alice, if there is anything within your own heart which is even a little akin to what I am speaking of? And if there is, might you consider accepting my courtship?"

It was such a long explanation that Alice could barely take it in. Her eyes flared, her breath caught though when Lord Sedgewick began to search her face, worry written into his features, she could not help but smile. Lord Sedgewick closed his eyes in clear relief and Alice settled one hand on his chest, bold now in her actions as the joy of their shared affection wrapped itself around her heart.

"I should like nothing more than to accept it, Sedgewick."

His eyes popped open.

"Truly?"

"Yes, truly!" Laughing softly, she found his hand with her free one and pressed her fingers through his. "Lord Sedgewick, I have found myself falling in love with you these last few weeks and have come now to a place where my affection for you is so great that I cannot even think to deny it. I have been afraid that I would not be truly seen by you, that my affection would be held only within my own heart, and not shared with you, but now, it seems, I am to be given all that I have longed for. I can hardly believe it!"

Lord Sedgewick chuckled and lifted their joined hands, pressing his lips to the back of her hand. Fire burned up her arm and Alice snatched in a breath, aware now of the desire to press her lips to his, rather than have his kiss to her hand – but now was not the moment for it. That would come. She simply had to be patient for a little longer.

"I have every intention of making our courtship a rather short one." Lord Sedgewick chuckled when her eyebrows lifted. "What I mean to say, Alice, is that my love for you is certain to grow with such speed, I will want nothing more than to make you my bride. I care not what society thinks nor about your father's disgrace. The only thing I care about is having you by my side."

Alice's happiness washed right through her, tears pricking her eyes as he kissed the back of her hand again.

"When that moment comes, I shall be glad to accept you," she promised, seeing him smile back into her eyes. "I have come to love you, Lord Sedgewick, and there is nothing that can ever separate my heart from yours."

"Then we shall be together for the rest of our days," he murmured, a tenderness in his expression which bound her all the tighter to him. "I cannot think of anything better."

. . .

So glad they found each other!

Did you miss the first book in the Waltzing with Wallflowers series The Wallflower's Unseen Charm Read ahead for a sneak peek of the story of a wallflower who can't keep quiet!

MY DEAR READER

Thank you for reading and supporting my books! I hope this story brought you some escape from the real world into the always captivating Regency world. A good story, especially one with a happy ending, just brightens your day and makes you feel good! If you enjoyed the book, would you leave a review on Amazon? Reviews are always appreciated.

Below is a complete list of all my books! Why not click and see if one of them can keep you entertained for a few hours?

The Duke's Daughters Series
The Duke's Daughters: A Sweet Regency Romance Boxset
A Rogue for a Lady
My Restless Earl
Rescued by an Earl
In the Arms of an Earl
The Reluctant Marquess (Prequel)

A Smithfield Market Regency Romance
The Smithfield Market Romances: A Sweet Regency Romance Boxset

The Rogue's Flower
Saved by the Scoundrel
Mending the Duke
The Baron's Malady

The Returned Lords of Grosvenor Square
The Returned Lords of Grosvenor Square: A Regency Romance Boxset
The Waiting Bride
The Long Return
The Duke's Saving Grace
A New Home for the Duke

The Spinsters Guild
The Spinsters Guild: A Sweet Regency Romance Boxset
A New Beginning
The Disgraced Bride
A Gentleman's Revenge
A Foolish Wager
A Lord Undone

Convenient Arrangements
Convenient Arrangements: A Regency Romance Collection
A Broken Betrothal
In Search of Love
Wed in Disgrace
Betrayal and Lies
A Past to Forget
Engaged to a Friend

Landon House
Landon House: A Regency Romance Boxset
Mistaken for a Rake
A Selfish Heart
A Love Unbroken
A Christmas Match
A Most Suitable Bride
An Expectation of Love

Second Chance Regency Romance
Second Chance Regency Romance Boxset
Loving the Scarred Soldier
Second Chance for Love
A Family of her Own
A Spinster No More

Soldiers and Sweethearts
To Trust a Viscount
Whispers of the Heart
Dare to Love a Marquess
Healing the Earl
A Lady's Brave Heart

Ladies on their Own: Governesses and Companions
Ladies on their Own Boxset
More Than a Companion
The Hidden Governess
The Companion and the Earl
More than a Governess
Protected by the Companion

Lost Fortunes, Found Love
A Viscount's Stolen Fortune
For Richer, For Poorer
Her Heart's Choice
A Dreadful Secret
Their Forgotten Love
His Convenient Match

Only for Love
The Heart of a Gentleman
A Lord or a Liar
The Earl's Unspoken Love
The Viscount's Unlikely Ally
The Highwayman's Hidden Heart
Miss Millington's Unexpected Suitor

Waltzing with Wallflowers
The Wallflower's Unseen Charm
The Wallflower's Midnight Waltz

Christmas Stories
The Uncatchable Earl
Love and Christmas Wishes: Three Regency Romance Novellas
A Family for Christmas
Mistletoe Magic: A Regency Romance
Heart, Homes & Holidays: A Sweet Romance Anthology

Christmas Kisses Series
Christmas Kisses Box Set
The Lady's Christmas Kiss

The Viscount's Christmas Queen
Her Christmas Duke

Happy Reading!
    All my love,
    Rose

A SNEAK PEEK OF THE WALLFLOWER'S UNSEEN CHARM

PROLOGUE

"You must promise me that you will *try*."

Miss Joy Bosworth rolled her eyes at her mother.

"Try to be more like my elder sisters, yes? That *is* what you mean, is it not?"

"And what is wrong with being like them?" Lady Halifax's stern tone told Joy in no uncertain terms that to criticize Bettina, Sarah, and Mary – all three of whom had married within the last few years – was a very poor decision indeed. Wincing, Joy fell silent and dropped her gaze to her lap as her beleaguered lady's maid continued to fix her hair. This was the third time that her lady's maid had set her hair, for the first two attempts had been deemed entirely unsuitable by Joy's mother – though quite what was wrong with it, Joy had been completely unable to see.

"You are much too forward, too quick to give your opinion," her mother continued, gazing at Joy's reflection in the looking glass, her eyes narrowing a little. "All of your elder sisters are quiet, though Bettina perhaps a little too much so, but their husbands greatly appreciate that about them! They speak when they are asked to speak, give their opinion when it is desired and otherwise say very little when it comes to matters which do not concern them. *You,* on the other hand, speak when you are *not* asked to do so, give your opinion most readily, and say a great deal on *any* subject even when it does not concern you!"

Hearing the strong emphasis, Joy chose not to drop her head further, as her mother might have expected, but instead to lift her chin and look back steadily. She was not about to be cowed when it came to such a trait. In some ways, she was rather proud of her determination to speak as she thought, for she was the only one of her sisters who did so. Mayhap it was simply because she was the youngest, but Joy did not truly know why - she had always been determined to speak up for herself and, simply because she was in London, was not, she thought, cause to alter herself now!

"You must find a suitable husband!" Exclaiming aloud, Lady Halifax threw up her hands, perhaps seeing the glint of steel in Joy's eyes. "Continuing to behave as you are will not attract anyone to you, I can assure you of that!"

"The *right* gentleman would still be attracted," Joy shot back, adding her own emphasis. "There must be some amongst society who do not feel the same way as you, Mother. I do not seek to disagree with you, only to suggest that there might be a little more consideration in some, or even a different viewpoint altogether!"

"I know what I am talking about!" Lady Halifax smote Joy gently on the shoulder though her expression was one of frustration. "I have already had three daughters wed and it would do you well to listen to me and my advice."

Joy did not know what to say. Yes, she had listened to her mother on many an occasion, but that did not mean that she had to take everything her mother said to heart... and on this occasion, she was certain that Lady Halifax was quite wrong.

"If I am not true to who I am, Mama, then will that not make for a very difficult marriage?"

"A difficult marriage?" This was said with such a degree of astonishment that Joy could not help but smile. "There is no such thing as a difficult marriage, not unless one of the two parties *within* the marriage itself attempts to make it so. Do you not understand, Joy? I am telling you to alter yourself so that you do *not* cause any difficulties, both for yourself now, and for your husband in the future."

The smile on Joy's face slipped and then blew away, her forehead furrowing as she looked at her mother again. Lady Halifax was everything a lady of quality ought to be, and she had trained each of her daughters to be as she was... except that Joy had never been the success her other daughters had been. Even now, the thought of stepping into marriage with a gentleman she barely knew, simply because he was deemed suitable, was rather horrifying to Joy, and was made all the worse by the idea that she would somehow have to pretend to be someone she was not!

"As I have said, Joy, you will try."

This time, Joy realized, it was not a question her mother had been asking her but a statement. A statement which said that she was expected to do nothing other than what her mother said – and to do so without question also.

I shall not lie.

"I think my hair is quite presentable now, Mama." Steadfastly refusing to either agree with or refuse what her mother had said, Joy sat up straight in her chair, her head lifting, her shoulders dropping low as she turned her head from side to side. "Very elegant, I must say."

"The ribbon is not the right color."

Joy resisted the urge to roll her eyes for what would be the second time.

"Mama, it is a light shade of green and it is threaded through the many braids Clara has tied my hair into. It is quite perfect and cannot be faulted. Besides, it does match the gown perfectly. You made certain of that yourself."

So saying, she threw a quick smile to her lady's maid and saw a twitch of Clara's lips before the maid bowed her head, stepping back so that Lady Halifax would not see the smile on her face.

"It is not quite as I would want it, but it will have to do." Lady Halifax sniffed and waved one hand in Clara's direction. "My daughter requires her gown now. And be quick about it, we are a little short on time."

"If you had not insisted that Clara do my hair on two further occasions, then we would not be in danger of being tardy," Joy remarked, rising from her chair, and walking across the room, quite missing the flash in her mother's eyes. "It was quite suitable the first time."

"*I* shall be the judge of that," came the sharp retort, as Lady Halifax stalked to the door. "Now do hurry up. The carriage is waiting, and I do not want us to bring the attention of the entire *ton* down upon us by walking in much later than any other!"

Joy sighed and nodded, turning back to where Clara was ready with her gown. Coming to London and seeking out a suitable match was not something she could get the least bit excited about, and this ball, rather than being a momentous one, filled with hope and expectation, felt like a heaviness on her shoulders. The sooner it was over, Joy considered, the happier she would be.

CHAPTER ONE

"And Lord Granger is seated there."

"Mm-hm."

Nudging Joy lightly, her mother scowled.

"You are not paying the least bit of attention! Instead, you are much too inclined towards staring! Though quite what you are staring at, I cannot imagine!"

Joy tilted her head but did not take her eyes away from what she had been looking at.

"I was wondering whether that lady there – the one with the rather ornate hairstyle – found it difficult to wear such a thing without difficulty or pain." The lady in question had what appeared to be a bird's nest of some description, adorned with feathers and lace, planted on one side of her head, with her hair going through it as though it were a part of the creation. There was also a bird sitting on the edge of the nest, though to Joy's eyes, it looked rather monstrous and not at all as it ought. "Surely it must be stuck to her head in some way." She could not keep a giggle back when the lady curtsied and then rose, only for her magnificent headpiece to wobble terribly. "Oh dear, perhaps it is not as well secured as it ought to be!"

"Will you stop speaking so loudly?"

The hiss from Lady Halifax had Joy's attention snapping back to her mother, a slight flush touching the edge of her cheeks as she realized that one or two of the other ladies near them were glancing in her direction. She had spoken a little too loudly for both her own good and her mother's liking.

"My apologies, Mama."

"I should think so!" Lady Halifax grabbed Joy's arm in a somewhat tight grip and then began to walk in the opposite direction of that taken by the lady with the magnificent hair. "Pray do not embarrass both me and yourself, with your hasty tongue!"

"I do not mean to," Joy muttered, allowing her mother to take her in whatever direction she wished. "I simply speak as I think."

"A trait I ought to have worked out of you by now, but instead, it seems determined to cling to you!" With a sigh, Lady Halifax shook her head. "Now look, do you see there?"

Coming to a hasty stop, Joy looked across the room, following the direction of her mother's gaze. "What is it that you wish me to look at, Mama?"

"Those young ladies there," came the reply. "Do you see them? They stand clustered together, hidden in the shadows of the ballroom. Even their own mothers or sponsors have given up on them!"

A frown tugged at Joy's forehead.

"I do not know what you are speaking of Mama."

"The wallflowers!" Lady Halifax turned sharply to Joy, her eyes flashing. "Do you not see them? They stand there, doing nothing other than adorning the wall. They are passed over constantly, ignored by the gentlemen of the *ton,* who care very little for their company."

"Then that is the fault of the gentlemen of the *ton,*" Joy answered, a little upset by her mother's remarks. "I do not think it is right to blame the young ladies for such a thing."

Lady Halifax groaned aloud, closing her eyes.

"Why do you willfully misunderstand? They are not wallflowers by choice, but because they are deemed as unsuitable for marriage, for one reason or another."

"Which, again, might not be their own doing."

"Perhaps, but all the same," Lady Halifax continued, sounding more exasperated than ever, "I have shown you these young ladies as a warning."

Joy's eyebrows shot towards her hairline.

"A warning?"

"Yes, that you will yourself become one such young lady if you do not begin to behave yourself and act as you ought." Moving so that she faced Joy directly, Lady Halifax narrowed her eyes a little. "You will find yourself standing there with them, doing nothing other than watching the gentlemen of London take various *other* young ladies out to dance, rather than showing any genuine interest in you. Would that not be painful? Would that not trouble you?"

The answer her mother wished her to give was evident to Joy, but she could not bring herself to say it. It was not that she wanted to cause her mother any pain, but that she could not permit herself to be false, not even if it would bring her a little comfort.

"It might," she admitted, eventually, as Lady Halifax let out another stifled groan, clearly exasperated. "But as I have said before, Mama, I do not wish to be courted by a gentleman who is unaware of my true nature. I do not see why I should hide myself away, simply so that I can please a suitor. If such a thing were to happen, if I were to be willing to act in that way, it would not make for a happy arrangement. Sooner or later, my real self would return to the fore, and then what would my husband do? It is not as though he could step back from our marriage. Therefore, I would be condemning both him and myself, to a life of misery. I do not think that would be at all agreeable."

"That is where you are wrong." Lady Halifax lifted her chin, though she looked straight ahead. "To be wed is the most satisfactory situation one can find oneself in, regardless of the circumstances. It is not as though you will spend a great deal of time with your husband so, therefore, you will never need to reveal your 'true nature', as you put it."

The more her mother talked, the more Joy found herself growing almost despondent, such was the picture Lady Halifax was painting of what would be waiting for her. She understood that yes, she was here to find a suitable match, but to then remove to her husband's estate, where she would spend most of her days alone and only be in her husband's company whenever he desired it, did not seem to Joy to be a very pleasant circumstance. That would be very dull indeed, would it not? Her existence would become small, insignificant, and utterly banal, and that was certainly *not* the future Joy wanted for herself.

"Now, do lift your head up, stand tall, and smile," came the command. "We must go and speak to Lord Falconer and Lord Dartford at once."

Joy hid her sigh by lowering her head, her eyes squeezing closed for a few moments. There was no time to protest, however, no time to explain to her mother that what had just been discussed had settled Joy's mind against such things as this, for Lady Halifax once more marched Joy across the room and, before she knew it, introduced Joy to the two gentlemen whom she had pointed out, as well as to one Lady Dartford, who was Lord Dartford's mother.

"Good evening." Joy rose from her curtsey and tried to smile, though her smile was a little lackluster. "How very glad I am to make your acquaintance."

"Said quite perfectly." Lord Dartford chuckled, his dark eyes sweeping across her features, then dropping down to her frame as Joy blushed furiously. "So, you are next in line to try your hand at the marriage mart?"

"Next in line?"

"Yes." Lord Dartford waved a hand as though to dismiss her words and her irritation, which Joy had attempted to make more than evident by the sweep of her eyebrow. "You have three elder sisters do you not?"

"Yes, I do." Joy kept her eyebrows lifted. "All of whom are all now wed and settled."

"And now you must do the same." Lord Dartford chuckled, but Joy did not smile. The sound was not a pleasant one. "Unfortunately, none of your sisters were able to catch my eye and, alas, I do not think that you will be able to do so either."

"Dartford!"

His mother's gasp of horror was clear, but Joy merely smiled, her stomach twisting at the sheer arrogance which the gentleman had displayed.

"That is a little forward of you, Lord Dartford," she remarked, speaking quite clearly, and ignoring the way that her mother set one hand to the small of her back in clear warning. "What is to say that I would have any interest in *your* company?"

This response wiped the smile from Lord Dartford's face. His dark eyes narrowed, and his jaw set but, much to Joy's delight, his friend began to guffaw, slapping Lord Dartford on the shoulder.

"You have certainly been set in your place!" Lord Falconer laughed as Joy looked back into Lord Dartford's angry expression without flinching. "And the lady is quite right, that was one of the most superior things I have heard you say this evening!"

"Only this evening?" Enjoying herself far too much, Joy tilted her head and let a smile dance across her features. "Again, Lord Dartford, I ask you what difference it would make to me to have a gentleman such as yourself interested in furthering their acquaintance with me? It is not as though I must simply accept every gentleman who comes to seek me out, is it? And I can assure you, I certainly would not accept you!"

Lord Falconer laughed again but Lord Dartford's

eyes narrowed all the more, his jaw tight and his frame stiff with clear anger and frustration.

"I do not think a young lady such as yourself should display such audacity, Miss Bosworth."

"And if I want your opinion, Lord Dartford, then I will ask you for it," Joy shot back, just as quickly. "Thus far, I do not recall doing so."

"We must excuse ourselves."

The hand that had been on Joy's back now turned into a pressing force that propelled her away from Lord Dartford, Lord Falconer, and Lady Dartford – the latter of whom was standing, staring at Joy with wide eyes, her face a little pale.

"Do excuse us."

Lady Halifax inclined her head and then took Joy's hand, grasping it tightly rather than with any gentleness whatsoever, dragging her away from the gentlemen she had only just introduced Joy to.

"Mama, you are hurting me!" Pulling her hand away, Joy scowled when her mother rounded on her. "Please, you must stop–"

"Do you know what you have done?"

The hissed words from her mother had Joy stopping short, a little surprised at her mother's vehemence.

"I have done nothing other than speak my mind and set Lord Dartford – someone who purports to be a gentleman – back into his place. I do not know what makes him think that I would have *any* interest in–"

"News of this will spread through London!" Lady Halifax blinked furiously, and it was only then that Joy saw the tears in her mother's eyes. "This is your very first ball on the eve of your come out, and you decide to speak with such force and impudence to the Earl of Dartford?"

A writhing began to roll itself around Joy's stomach.

"I do not know what you mean. I did nothing wrong."

"It is not about wrong or right," came the reply, as Lady Halifax whispered with force towards Joy. "It is about wisdom. You did not speak with any wisdom this evening, and now news of what you did will spread throughout society. Lady Dartford will see to that."

Joy lifted her shoulders and then let them fall.

"I could not permit Lord Dartford to speak to me in such a way. I am worthy of respect, am I not?"

"You could have ignored him!" Lady Halifax threw up her hands, no longer managing to maintain her composure, garnering the attention of one or two others nearby. "You did not have to say a single thing! A simple look – or a slight curl of the lip – would have sufficed. Instead, you did precisely what I told you not to do and now news of your audacity will spread through London. Lady Dartford is one of the most prolific gossips in all of London and given that you insulted her son, I fear for what she will say."

Joy kept her chin lifted.

"Mama, Lady Dartford was shocked at her own son's remarks to me."

"But that does not mean that she will speak of *him* in the same way that she will speak of you," Lady Halifax told her, a single tear falling as red spots appeared on her cheeks. "Do you not understand, Joy?"

"Lord Falconer laughed at what I said."

Lady Halifax closed her eyes.

"That means nothing, other than the fact that he found your remarks and your behavior to be mirthful. It will not save your reputation."

"I did nothing to ruin my reputation."

"Oh, but you did." A flash came into her mother's eyes. "You may not see it as yet, but I can assure you, you have done yourself a great deal of damage. I warned you, I *asked* you to be cautious and instead, you did the opposite. Now, within the first ball of the Season, your sharp tongue and your determination to speak as you please has brought you into greater difficulty than you can imagine." Her eyes closed, a heavy sigh breaking from her. "Mayhap you will become a wallflower after all."

Hmm, my mother always said my mouth would get me into trouble...and now Miss Bosworth could be in trouble! Check out the rest of the story on the Kindle store The Wallflower's Unseen Charm

JOIN MY MAILING LIST

Sign up for my newsletter to stay up to date on new releases, contests, giveaways, freebies, and deals!

Free book with signup!

Monthly Facebook Giveaways! Books and Amazon gift cards!
Join me on Facebook: https://www.facebook.com/rosepearsonauthor

Website: www.RosePearsonAuthor.com

Follow me on Goodreads: Author Page

You can also follow me on Bookbub!
Click on the picture below – see the Follow button?

230 | JOIN MY MAILING LIST

Printed in Great Britain
by Amazon